DEATH WALKS
THE WOODS

DEATH WALKS THE WOODS

CYRIL HARE

HarperPerennial
A Division of HarperCollins*Publishers*

First Perennial Library edition published 1981. First Harper-Perennial edition published 1991.

LIBRARY OF CONGRESS CATALOG CARD NUMBER 91-55153

ISBN 0-06-092136-6

91 92 93 94 95 MB 10 9 8 7 6 5 4 3 2 1

Contents

1

A Room with a View

Francis Pettigrew started guiltily as his wife came into the room. At his own particular request he had been left undisturbed for the whole morning in order to prepare his lecture to the Mid-Markshire Law Society on "Modern Trends in the Theory of Torts". Now he was uncomfortably conscious of the fact that for the last half-hour he had been staring out of the window.

"How is it going?" asked Eleanor with an air of solicitude in which her husband's quick ear detected a hint of irony.

"It is not going at all, and well you know it," he said.

"I don't see why I should know anything of the sort, Frank. You haven't had anything to disturb you, I hope?"

"Disturb?" Pettigrew looked up from his untidy desk and out of the window again. "Tell me, what did your uncle do while he lived here?"

"Uncle Robert? Well, nothing so far as I know. He had retired, of course. I know he always intended to write a book about his travels, but somehow it never got finished."

"You are wrong. It never got started. And I will tell you just why. Your Uncle Robert wasted the time he meant to have spent in writing just as I have spent this morning—looking at the view."

Eleanor laughed. "I believe he did," she said. "But Uncle Robert was a rather weak character, I'm afraid."

"So, no doubt, am I. But I don't believe any character, however strong, could stand up to a distraction like that. It is all nonsense to talk of surroundings like these being conducive to work. They are positively lethal to any kind of endeavour. That is why all the best writers have lived in garrets when they weren't in prison."

"Frank, you're simply making excuses for your idleness. You forget that Yew Hill is famous for its writers. Henry Spicer, for instance."

"Spicer proves my point exactly. He lived down *there*." Pettigrew pointed downwards to the valley beneath the window. "He went for long walks on the hill and then came back to his cottage in the bottom to write his poetry and his interminable romances. You can't see a hundred yards from his windows. If he had lived here he'd never have put pen to paper."

"It *is* a lovely view." Eleanor, too, was now gazing out of the window. After a long silence she said, "The wild cherry is beginning to show up wonderfully against the yews, isn't it?"

"There are three more trees out today than there were yesterday. I've been keeping count.... What's the name of that odd-looking house almost round the corner at the top?"

"The Alps. I don't know who lives there now. It used to be old Lady Fothergill when I was a child. She kept Great Danes which terrified us.... Look, Frank, there are some very odd-looking people coming down the slope now."

Pettigrew reached for the field-glasses which stood ready on his desk.

"Americans," he pronounced. "Poppa, Momma and two very weirdly dressed boys. Pop's got what looks like a guide-book in his hand. Momma's heels are much too high for comfort. I suppose they've left their car at the top."

"Do let me see." Eleanor took the glasses from him.

"What's the betting they're on a literary pilgrimage to Spicer's cottage?...There, what did I tell you? They've taken the path down to the left."

Eleanor had shifted her gaze to another part of the hill.

"Two people coming up the other way," she said. "They seem to be looking for something. One's carrying a vasculum. What do you suppose they can be after? It's much too early for the orchids...."

She put down the glasses, and it could be observed that she was blushing slightly.

"I came in to say that lunch was ready," she said.

"There you are," said her husband brutally. "Now it is burnt, or chilled, or whatever happens to lunch when the cook takes times off to admire the view. If it wasn't for the lucky fact that the kitchen looks out at the back we should get no meals at all. I tell you, you should never have persuaded me to come and live here. It is utterly demoralizing for both of us."

In high good humour he followed his wife from the room. A draught from the open window scattered the pages of the unfinished lecture about the floor.

Yew Hill, Markshire, was well known to lovers of the picturesque long before Henry Spicer, that revered but now largely unread giant of Victorian letters, put it firmly upon the literary map of England. Since his day the growth of modern transport has made it accessible to the world at large, and it would be hard to name a better-known beauty spot anywhere within fifty miles of London. Spicer it was whose verses first associated the huge and ancient yew trees that fringe its sides with Druidic rites. Nowadays, the Druids Hotel, conveniently placed on the arterial road to Markhampton, is one of the best properties of its class in the southern counties. On any fine week-end the bare, grassy slopes of the hill are dotted with parties of happy tourists who would have driven that surly recluse to distraction, and the

3

yews he celebrated spread their branches over couples contentedly unburdened by any acquaintance with the works of Spicer, and often occupied in rites considerably older than the Druids.

The hill lies in the parish of Yewbury, a village tucked snugly away in the valley and nearly a mile distant. Except for a solitary like Henry Spicer or an eccentric like the late Sir William Fothergill, nobody in the past would wish to build on the hill, where the soil barely covered the barren chalk and the water supply was problematical. The National Trust sees to it that nobody shall do so in the future. But on the other side of the valley, where the ground rises more gently towards the lesser eminence of Didbury Down, a small colony of houses—known unofficially as East Yewbury—has established itself in recent years, beneficiaries of the wreck of the bankrupt Earl of Markshire's once great estate. These the house agents are wont to advertise as "commanding unrivalled views of Yew Hill". If Pettigrew's experience was anything to go upon, it was in fact the view that commanded them.

Francis Pettigrew was by habit and inclination an urban character. His working life had been spent in the Temple, where the prospect from his chambers was bounded by an elegant piece of seventeenth-century brickwork, twenty paces away. (When German bombs, by blasting away the opposite side of the Court, extended his view overnight to the further side of the river, he had felt as lost as a caged canary suddenly let loose in a forest.) His knowledge of the country was mainly confined to the Assize towns of the Southern Circuit, and a small house in the centre of Markhampton had seemed to him the obvious place to select for his retirement.

He had reckoned without his wife—the young woman whom he had so unexpectedly—and so fortunately—acquired as a pendant to his government service during the Second World War. More particularly, he had reckoned without his wife's aunt—a widow whom he had never met and of whom he had barely heard. When this lady eventually died, after lingering on the

4

verge of imbecility for many years, it was found that she had left her niece, along with the rest of her property, the tiny house in which he now found himself. He had assumed that they would dispose of the place, and had come with Eleanor to examine it as a matter of form. He took one look from the study windows, wondered what he had been doing with his eyes all his life, and surrendered at discretion. The discovery of Uncle Robert's pair of Zeiss binoculars, still in excellent condition, completed his discomfiture.

"Unless something pretty drastic happens to me here," he remarked to his wife at lunch, "I am going to become completely torpid."

"Lady Furlong has rung up to ask if she can come to tea," said Eleanor. "Perhaps that will be drastic enough."

Lady Furlong was the doyenne of East Yewbury. Spiritually she belonged to the established community of Yewbury proper, and her mission in life was to see that any newcomers were brought in to play their proper part in parish affairs. A distant connection of Lord Markshire's family, she insensibly assumed proprietary airs in all that appertained to the neighbourhood, and long before tea was over Pettigrew found it difficult not to succumb to the illusion that he was a humble tenant under the inspection of his landlord, and not a landed proprietor—or at least the husband of one—entertaining another whose holding was scarcely larger than his own.

But Lady Furlong, if inclined to be dictatorial, was amiable enough, and the fact that Eleanor had come into her little property by inheritance and not by purchase was sufficient to raise her in her regard. When it further transpired that she had spent part of her childhood in the house with her uncle and aunt and had actually for a brief period attended the same infants' school as Lady Furlong's elder son the atmosphere became positively cordial. Eleanor had been "placed", and from that moment her ladyship was entirely at her ease. She spent a great deal of her time in an endeavour, becoming yearly more and more difficult in a world increasingly disturbed, to "place" people properly, and she was obviously overjoyed that in this case the task had been so easy, and the result so satisfactory. Accepting a third cup of tea, she settled down to business. Had Eleanor met the Vicar yet? No? The Vicar would call. He was a little concerned about helpers for the summer bazaar. Perhaps Eleanor would care to take charge of a stall? Well, possibly it was rather early in the day to consider that, but she must think it over. Lady Furlong was seeing Mrs. Pink that evening and they would run over the list of workers and see where she could be most useful. Then, of course there was the Women's Institute....

Eleanor expressed an unexpected yearning to join the Women's Institute, provided its meetings did not clash with rehearsals of the Markhampton Orchestral Society, to which she remained faithful. Happily they did not, and Lady Furlong beamed with pleasure at her new recruit. Mrs. Pink would send her a list of meetings. She went on to press the claims of the Moral Welfare Association, and of the newly formed Friends of Yew Hill, designed to preserve that landmark from the vandalism of certain of the summer visitors.

Pettigrew's head began to whirl. He had pictured Yewbury as a haven of rest, but it seemed that instead it was a vortex of activity beside which a beehive would look positively stagnant. Before long, he learned that, unlike a beehive, Yewbury exacted work from both sexes. The British Legion had a branch there. Lady Furlong would mention Pettigrew's name to Colonel Sampson, just up the lane. He was just the type they would welcome on the committee. The Colonel was the local secretary, a most valuable man. So conscientious, too. He had even taken typing lessons to try to keep up with his work. Fortunately that was no longer necessary, now that Mrs. Pink had taken on the clerical side.

"Who is Mrs. Pink?" Pettigrew ventured to ask. He had noticed that she was the branch secretary of the Moral Welfare

Association, besides being treasurer of the Friends of Yew Hill. "She seems to be a very important person. Is she the Vicar's wife?"

"Good gracious, no!" Lady Furlong permitted herself a short laugh at his ignorance. "The Vicar is a bachelor—thank goodness. As to *important*—I should hardly call Mrs. Pink that. But she is a very good, worthy, *useful* person." (If Mrs. Pink isn't placed after that series of adjectives, thought Pettigrew, she never will be.) "Indeed I don't know how I ever managed without her. She has only been in the village three or four years, but already she has made herself quite indispensable. A widow, of course, and entirely given up to good works."

Mrs. Pink disposed of, Lady Furlong rose to go. Pettigrew showed her out.

"You have quite a good view from here," she observed with a touch of condescension from the porch. "It is not quite the same as mine, of course. From my windows I see much more of the Druids' Glade and rather less of the bare slope. I think it is preferable, seen that way. One is less conscious of the trippers."

"That reminds me," said Pettigrew. "Who lives in the house at the top of the hill—The Alps, I think it is called?"

"Oh...Mrs. Ransome," said Lady Furlong. "I don't somehow think your wife will want to meet her. Goodbye, Mr. Pettigrew. So very glad to have made your acquaintance."

She climbed into her antique two-seater, leaving Pettigrew in no doubt whatever that Mrs. Ransome, so far from being placed, was low down among the also ran.

"By the way," Lady Furlong called from the car, "I forgot to mention it to your wife, but if you require a chicken at any time Mr. Wendon is your man. The smallholding at the bottom of the hill."

"I think I have seen him," said Pettigrew. "A rather weedy type with fair hair?"

"That is the man. Mention my name and he will look you out

a good one. I like to help him when I can. It's odd to think, isn't it,"—she lowered her voice to reveal the distressing fact—"that he was actually at Harrow with my nephew."

Shaking her head sadly at a state of affairs in which people failed so dismally to keep their place, she drove away.

Pettigrew was still admiring the effect of the evening light on the hill when he heard the telephone ring. He turned to go indoors and met Eleanor coming out for him.

"Somebody wants to speak to you," she said. "He says he's the Lord Chancellor's office."

She seemed to be impressed by the august name, but her husband shrugged his shoulders indifferently.

"Once upon a time a message like that would have sent me crazy with excitement," he said. "But at my age it's too late to expect anything much from that quarter. However..."

He went in and picked up the receiver.

"Pettigrew here.... Oh, is he? I'm sorry to hear it. Not bad, I hope?...I see. Yes, I can manage it all right. Where, did you say?...Didford? That's quite accessible. I'll be there.... Yes, I'll let you have an account of my expenses.... Very well. Goodbye."

He rang off with an odd expression, half bitter and half amused. Then he sat down and burst out laughing.

"What is all this about?" asked Eleanor.

"Jefferson is ill. They've just rushed him off to hospital with a duodenal ulcer."

"That doesn't sound terribly funny. Who is this poor Mr. Jefferson?"

. "He's not a mister. He's the County Court Judge of this district. They want me to sit as his deputy. Seven guineas a day and expenses, starting at Didford tomorrow. As you say, it's not a bit funny. But all the same——"

Pettigrew blew his nose, wiped his spectacles and became serious again.

"Twelve—no, thirteen years ago I put in for that job," he said. "They turned me down, largely, I believe, because I was getting a bit long in the tooth and was considered rather a crock. If they'd taken me instead of him I should have nearly earned my pension by now. And now Jefferson has cracked up and they want me to sit for him. Isn't life odd?"

He looked out of the window at the long ridge of Yew Hill, hard and clear against the darkening sky.

"I shall miss this while I'm in court," he said. "But, anyway, it will be one way of meeting some of our neighbours."

2

Mendelism in the County Court

Didford, or to give it its full name Didford Parva—Didford Magna being a minute and forgotten village farther up the valley—is a small market town, the shopping and business centre of the district in which Yewbury lies. It is the centre also of such judicial business as the neighbourhood provides. The felonies and misdemeanours of the inhabitants are normally disposed of at a weekly session of the local justices, and their civil disputes are barely sufficient to justify a visit from the County Court Judge once a month. The newly appointed deputy, as he took his seat in the shabby courtroom, felt that he was being given an easy initiation into the mysteries of judging. The list of cases for hearing was short, and besides the half-dozen or so solicitors at the table there were not more than twenty people present.

"Judgment summonses," snapped the clerk from below the bench. "Spokes against Grantley."

He turned and thrust a blue paper on to the judge's desk, a very stout, elderly man who looked like a tramp waddled into the witness-box, and the business of the day had begun almost before Pettigrew was aware of it.

A hatchet-faced solicitor rose.

"For the creditor, your honour. Mr. Grantley, you owe five hundred and nineteen pounds. How can you pay?"

"Pound a month," said Mr. Grantley calmly.

"*How* much?" gasped Pettigrew.

Evidently taking the deputy to be hard of hearing, the creditor's representative thundered: "He offers a pound a month. Will your honour make it thirty shillings?"

"Yes, if you like," said Pettigrew feebly.

The stout man nodded curtly and waddled slowly out of court. Everybody seemed perfectly satisfied. Pettigrew stared after him, wondering by what hidden magic he had ever attracted credit for £519. Mr. Grantley, he reflected, was now sixty, if a day. How old would he be by the time the debt was finally settled at this generous rate? He was trying to work it out in his head when he was aware that the blue paper had disappeared and another taken its place.

"Ingleson against Wates," said the clerk.

The hatchet-faced solicitor was on his feet again.

"The debtor isn't here, your honour. Adjourn to the next court for the usual letter to be sent?"

"By all means," said Pettigrew. Really, this job was easy. He must remember to ask the clerk what the usual letter was.

Three or four more debtors succeeded one another rapidly in the box. They all appeared to owe sums immensely disproportionate to their earnings, none had less than four young children to support and their debts were mainly in respect of such bare necessities of life as television sets and suites of dining-room furniture. Their creditors—or at least the creditors' legal representatives—gladly accepted offers which promised them repayment in an average period of twenty-five years, provided the instalments were maintained.

"Why I've wasted time and energy paying bills all my life," mused Pettigrew, "I simply can't imagine." He directed another usual letter to be sent, and then sat up in interest as a familiar name was called.

"Meal and Malt Limited against Wendon."

The blue paper recorded a judgment with costs amounting to £25 12s. 8d.

"Mr. Wendon, how can you pay this debt?"

Mr. Wendon did not offer a pound, or any other sum, a month. Instead, he turned a pair of candid blue eyes towards the bench, and observed:

"The fact is, your honour, the meal was rotten bad. Positively mouldy."

"That isn't the point," interjected the solicitor—not the hatchet-faced one this time, but the florid one with a moustache, who appeared to share with the other the major part of this unrewarding practice. "Not the point at all. You have a judgment against you——"

"I nearly lost three young gilts over it," went on Mr. Wendon. "Had to call in the vet. I still owe him a fiver for the job."

It was easy to believe, hearing him speak, that Horace Wendon had been at Harrow with Lady Furlong's nephew. In appearance, however, he scarcely did credit to that, or any other, public school. He was perhaps a little better dressed than Mr. Grantley, but only a very little, and he was considerably dirtier. A faint odour of pig manure was wafted from the witness-box. The face was not without distinction, but bore the unmistakable expression of a man with a grievance—a grievance which he was resigned never to see remedied.

"Just let me get this clear," said Pettigrew. "I gather that this bill is for meal supplied to you——"

"If you can call it meal—yes."

"—which you didn't pay for."

"Well, naturally not. I mean, would you?"

"Never mind about me for the moment. You were sued for the debt?"

"That's right."

"Did you tell the judge that the meal was bad?"

12

"Tell the judge? No, I wasn't there. I had a sow due to farrow that day, I think. Anyhow, I didn't turn up."

"And you didn't think it worth while to consult a solicitor about the business?"

"Solicitor?" Mr. Wendon's face was a study in contempt. "No thanks. I've had some."

"Then I'm afraid you'll have to pay."

"If *you* say so," said Mr. Wendon wearily. He seemed to abandon the contest almost with relief, as though the effort of protesting against ill usage was too much for him. "But you ought to have seen that meal," he added.

"And now, Mr. Wendon," said the florid solicitor, who had been champing, metaphorically at the bit and literally at his moustache during this colloquy, "how can you pay this debt?"

"Well, that's just the point, isn't it? I mean, how?"

"You're a farmer, aren't you?"

"I prefer to say smallholder, myself."

"Married?"

"Good Lord, no."

"What's your rent?"

"Don't pay any."

"You own your place?"

"Sort of. There's a mortgage on it, of course."

"Got a bank account?"

"Overdrawn."

"Any other debts?"

"Nothing to speak of. There's the vet., of course."

"Any money owing to you?"

There was a perceptible pause before this question was answered.

"Yes, there is."

"How much?"

"Eight thousand three hundred and fourteen pounds."

Wendon had the figures pat, like a child repeating a lesson.

Watching him, Pettigrew realized that the grievance which he had divined at first sight of the man had come to the surface. He longed to know the story behind it, but the pace was too hot to enquire.

"And when do you expect to be paid?"

Wendon's look of resignation deepened. "Never," he said.

"Then don't waste his honour's time. What is your monthly profit, do you think?...Do you pay income-tax?...Do you...? Have you...?"

At long last, after a contest which reminded Pettigrew of a pertinacious but clumsy terrier chasing an extremely elusive rat, Mr. Wendon was driven to admit that he could afford to pay two pounds a month. His departure marked the end of the judgment summonses, and the actions down for trial then began.

The present condition of the inhabitants of Markshire, as reflected in the business of the County Courts, consists, like that of the rest of the United Kingdom, in too many people chasing after too few houses. Nowadays, nobody who has once admitted anyone else into his home on any terms whatever can hope to get him or her out again without going to court about it. Pettigrew was not in the least surprised to find that all the cases in his list were of the type known to the trade as "possession cases". The first batch were simple enough, from the legal point of view, since the hapless defendants were merely holding on in the hope that once an order for eviction was made against them somebody, somewhere, somehow, would find them a place to go to. In rapid succession Pettigrew dealt with the case of the cowman's widow with a long string of children who must make way for her husband's successor if the business of the farm was to be carried on; of the young married couple who had disastrously overstayed their welcome in the tiny, overcrowded cottage of the husband's parents; of the butler in the big house whose employer's death had left him bewildered and unprotected in a world that did not want butlers and proposed to turn the big house into an institution for mental defectives. These preliminaries over—at what cost in anxiety and suffering Pettigrew did not care to think—the decks were cleared for the main work of the day, the seriously contested actions.

"A straightforward hardship case, your honour," said the plaintiff's advocate cheerfully when the first of these cases was called. Pettigrew groaned within himself. Paragraph 12 (I) (h) of the First Schedule to the Act—he knew it by heart already. This was one of those desperate cases in which he, Pettigrew, he and no other, would have to decide whether greater hardship would be inflicted on the tenant by turning him out or on the landlord by keeping *him* out of a house. He expected the worst, and the worst was duly forthcoming. The case for the landlord was positively heartrending. So atrocious was the hardship under which he and his family were labouring that Pettigrew caught himself wondering how any tenant could have the effrontery to resist such an overwhelming claim. He did not wonder long. The defendant's solicitor, when his turn came, produced evidence of the appalling cataract of misfortune which would descend upon his clients if they lost their foothold in the coveted dwelling (two sitting-rooms, two bedrooms and boxroom, scullery and outside W.C.). It was unthinkable that they should be evicted—but Pettigrew was compelled to think of it.

Before the case was over six doctor's certificates lay on his desk. Four testified to the dangerous ailments under which both parties and their respective wives were labouring. The other two announced the imminent arrival of new members in each of the two families. Whichever side was successful, the two bedrooms and boxroom would have to accommodate at least twice as many people as they had been designed for. Whichever lost would presumably have to camp out on Didbury Down. Such, social historians of the future please note, were the housing conditions of Markshire in the year of grace 1952.

He decided the case somehow—in whose favour he did not afterwards care to think. He only knew that he had not done justice, simply because justice was not possible in the circumstances— unless it is just to punish blameless people for living in a time and

15

at a place where there is no room for them. Then he went out to lunch, reflecting guiltily on his own snug quarters, with a dressing-room to himself and a spare room for the chance visitor.

"Todman *v.* Pink" headed the list for the afternoon's work. Todman was represented by the hatchet-faced man of law, whose name, somewhat unexpectedly, proved to be Lovely. Pink appeared in person. It was not until the defendant came forward in answer to the summons that Pettigrew, preoccupied as he was with the prospect of another "hardship case", realized that this must be the good, worthy, useful person of whom Lady Furlong had spoken. He looked at her with interest. He was surprised to note that she was a comparatively young woman, not more than forty, at most. In view of Lady Furlong's adjectives he had expected to see someone on the wrong side of fifty, though why such qualities should necessarily belong to middle age it would be hard to say. She was not particularly good-looking, and her dress, to Pettigrew's inexpert eye, in no way differed from that of the ordinary, hardworking village woman. But there was some-thing about her appearance that compelled attention. Casting about for a definition, Pettigrew found himself hitting on the word "dignity". It was the dignity, not of self-assurance or con-ceit—at the moment Mrs. Pink looked extremely nervous and unassuming—but of unassailable integrity. "Good, worthy, use-ful," he thought. "I am sure she is all that—but especially good."

It was time to listen to Mr. Lovely. He seemed extremely con-fident of his case, and there appeared to be every reason for his confidence. His client, Mr. Jesse Todman, whom Pettigrew already knew by sight as the proprietor of Yewbury's only garage and petrol station, desired possession of his cottage for his daughter and son-in-law, recently married, with a child on the way, and now living in the usual circumstances of squalor in one room over Mr. Todman's garage.

"I don't expect your honour will find very much difficulty in this case," said Mr. Lovely. "Mrs. Pink is a widow, I understand, without dependants, living by herself, and occupying this four-

16

roomed house. She should have no difficulty in finding somewhere sufficient for her simple needs. On the other hand, here is this young couple anxious to make a home of their own, and, of course, living in conditions in which I am sure your honour will feel it would be most undesirable to bring up a young family. My client is not without sympathy for Mrs. Pink, but ..."

When Mr. Todman came into the witness-box he very successfully disguised the sympathy for his tenant with which Mr. Lovely had so generously credited him. He was a small, wiry man with bright yellow hair and hard, grey eyes. Yes, he owned the cottage—had inherited it from his father just after Mrs. Pink went in—at a rent, he added gratuitously, that showed him no profit, after paying for the repairs the sanitary man had made him do. He had been asking her to go ever since. Now his daughter's husband had come out of the army, there wasn't room for them all in his house, and that, his expression said plainly, was that.

Pettigrew turned to Mrs. Pink.

"Would you like to ask Mr. Todman any questions?" he said.

"No, thank you, sir."

For good measure, Mr. Lovely went on to call Mrs. Todman, a tall, lymphatic blonde who just couldn't manage with a married daughter in the house, and as for a baby—well, there simply wouldn't be room to turn round with nappies all over the place, would there? There being once more no questions from Mrs. Pink, she was succeeded immediately in the box by her daughter.

The daughter, named, according to modern Markshire fashion, Marlene Deirdre Banks, was only too plainly an expectant mother. Regarding her, Pettigrew could only hope that, in case of need, the court bailiff, a competent-looking man and an obvious ex-policeman, would prove to have added a course in midwifery to his other qualifications. But she survived her brief appearance as a witness without disaster and left Pettigrew with a comparatively agreeable impression of a pair of very bright brown eyes and a shock of untidy dark hair.

Marlene's evidence concluded the plaintiff's case. Pettigrew turned to Mrs. Pink.

"Now I should like to hear what you have to say," he said as kindly as he could.

He knew only too well what she was going to say, and his heart smote him as he looked at that quiet, patient face. Mrs. Pink had nowhere to go. Obviously not. Nobody had nowadays. But what would that avail her against Marlene's pregnancy and the patent impossibility of rearing her child in the shanty over her father's garage? The case was as good as decided already and it was only a question of how long he could allow her, in the beautifully vague phrase, "to make other arrangements". How he would ever dare to face Lady Furlong after this he did not care to think.

"I am sorry to be such a trouble to everybody," said Mrs. Pink. "But the fact is, I have nowhere to go. It is very difficult to find anywhere to live in Yewbury," she added.

"Quite," said Pettigrew encouragingly, but no further words came. Mrs. Pink had put her defence in the fewest possible words.

And there the cause of Todman v. Pink would have ended, had not Mr. Lovely, anxious to justify his fee, been inspired to cross-examine.

"You've got this house all to yourself, haven't you?" he said accusingly. "A four-roomed house!" His tone of voice somehow gave the cottage the amplitude of a Blenheim Palace. "You don't want all that space, surely?"

"Oh, but I do—really I do."

"Why can't you go and live in a furnished room somewhere?"

"That wouldn't really be possible, I'm afraid. I have so many things to look after."

"Things? You could store your furniture, I suppose?"

"It isn't only the furniture," Mrs. Pink explained gently. "There are all my papers—I do so much work. It wouldn't really be suitable in a furnished room."

Pettigrew had a sudden vision of a village landlady prying

18

into the confidential correspondence of the Moral Welfare Association. No, it would not be suitable. Well, Lady Furlong would have to find another secretary, that was all. A pity, but——

Mr. Lovely was still developing his theme.

"A widow without encumbrances—that's you, Mrs. Pink, isn't it?" Receiving no reply, he went on, "You have nobody else to share this four-roomed house with, have you?"

"No. That is—nobody, now." The last word was spoken hardly above a whisper.

"Very well. Now have you seriously considered finding other accommodation, madam? Have you made any enquiries as to the possibility of purchasing a residence?"

(In the County Court, Pettigrew reflected, we always purchase residences. We leave it to lesser breeds without the law to buy houses.)

"I could not possibly afford it."

"Are you sure, madam? You can get very easy terms from building societies nowadays. You have enjoyed a very low rent for some years. Have you no savings?"

"Very small ones."

"Just how much money have you? What is your income?"

A look of acute distress passed over Mrs. Pink's face.

This really isn't fair, thought Pettigrew. She must feel as if she was being undressed in public.

"Perhaps you would prefer to write it down," he suggested.

"Thank you, sir." Mrs. Pink was handed pencil and paper, and after a little anxious calculation she wrote down two figures, representing capital and income respectively. Pettigrew looked at them and then handed the paper down to Mr. Lovely. As he had expected, they were pitifully small.

"And that is all you have?" Mr. Lovely persisted.

"That is all the money in the world at my disposition."

She dropped the stilted words into the court like pebbles into a calm pool, wrapping her strange dignity round her like a cloak.

Mr. Lovely was off on another tack.

"There is no particular reason why you should live in Yewbury, is there?" he asked. "You could go to any other part of Markshire equally well—to any other part of England, for the matter of that?"

Then for the first time Mrs. Pink became vocal, almost eloquent. "That is perfectly true, in a sense, I suppose," she said. "I am attached to my work in Yewbury, of course, but I expect I could find myself useful things to do wherever I lived. I have always made myself useful wherever I was, thank God. It isn't only that, sir. I am very fond of Yewbury, you see. I was born there. I lived there until I went away to get married. That's why I came back when—when I was left alone." For a moment she seemed to have forgotten where she was. She went on speaking, half to Pettigrew, half to herself, borne on a stream of childhood memories. "My father was the organist in Yewbury Church. He used to let me sit in the organ loft with him when I was a little girl. I loved it. I don't suppose he was a very good performer, really, but I thought his playing the most wonderful thing in the world." She looked round, past Mr. Lovely to the bench behind him where the plaintiff and his family were sitting. "He played at your wedding, Mr. Todman," she said. "Do you remember? It's a long time ago, but I can see it all as plain as plain. There were four bridesmaids in blue, and Mrs. Potts wore pink. She was a lovely bride, for all we thought her a little tall for you…"

Really, the deputy judge felt, this was all most irregular. Jefferson would have stopped her long ago. He cleared his throat to intervene, but Mrs. Pink had stopped of her own accord. She was now dabbing at her eyes with a handkerchief. Mr. Lovely, shrugging his shoulders, sat down and began to tie up his papers. Quite clearly, the case was over. Pettigrew drew breath to announce his decision.

It was at this precise moment that Pettigrew felt rising strongly within him a suspicion that things were not altogether what they seemed. He paused, wrinkling his nose like a dog sniffing at a faint, elusive scent. There was something odd about this apparently simple little case, if he could only put his finger on it. Something he had casually observed during the hearing and not properly attended to at the time. That and something else Mrs. Pink had let fall in her rambling remarks. He looked round the silent court in search of inspiration. His eye lit on the Todmans, sitting together, with Marlene's tousled brown wig close against her mother's shoulder. A vague memory of a textbook on Mendelism came to him, and the two ideas suddenly coalesced in his mind and ran together like raindrops on a window-pane.

"I'd like Mr. Todman to come back into the witness-box," he said.

Surprised and annoyed, Mr. Todman came forward once more.

"Just two questions," said Pettigrew. "Was your wife a widow when you married her?"

"That's right."

"Is Mrs. Banks your daughter, or the child of the earlier marriage?"

"My Marlene," said Mr. Todman emphatically, "has never known any other father but me."

"Quite. But that's not exactly——"

"I gave her my home. I gave her my name. That was twenty-two years ago. She was a baby then, and twelve months old. What more could a man do?"

Pettigrew was reading yet once again the familiar words of Paragraph 12(h) of the First Schedule. They were as he had thought.

"You did not adopt her legally?"

"No."

Pettigrew looked at Mr. Lovely. Mr. Lovely rose to his feet. He had the expression of a boxer coming out of his corner in the certain knowledge that he is going to be knocked out in the next few moments.

"Can you get round this difficulty?" Pettigrew asked him.

21

"The Act states specifically that the house must be required by the landlord as a residence for himself or any son or daughter *of his*. I see no mention of stepdaughters."

Mr. Lovely was too good a lawyer to waste time arguing an impossible proposition. He put up only a token resistance and admitted defeat. He was, naturally, concerned to point out that he had conducted the case upon the footing that Mrs. Banks was in fact Mr. Todman's daughter. Pettigrew, equally naturally, accepted his assurance, while privately wondering that a man of his obvious intelligence should not have known that by the laws of genetics two blondes do not make a brown. He had already conveniently forgotten that he would have overlooked the fact himself if Mrs. Pink had not given him the hint.

"There will be judgment for the defendant," he said. He felt the lawyer's satisfaction at arriving at an unassailable decision on a plain point of law, which, like the Order of the Garter, had no damned merit about it.

None the less, when, half an hour later, he was on his way home he felt on reflection that there was still something unsatisfactory about the odd little drama that had been played out before him. It is seldom that any judge really gets to the bottom of a case. The well of truth is usually too deep for the merely judicial plumb-line. Pettigrew was morally certain that he had not reached the bottom of this one. That by itself would not have worried him. What he found really disturbing was his conviction that during the course of the proceedings Mrs. Pink had more than once—not lied exactly, but faltered with the truth. And since Mrs. Pink had impressed him as a woman of exceptionally high character, it left him puzzled, and even a little distressed on her account.

3

Mrs. Pink at Home

Mrs. Pink left the town hall just too late to catch the half-past three bus from the market-place and she was condemned to a thirty-minutes wait for the next one. Nobody, looking at her as she stood at the head of a slowly lengthening queue, would have taken her for a successful litigant—least of all for one whose success had been as complete as it had been unexpected. She was tired, hungry and dispirited. Her head ached and she was badly in need of a nice hot cup of tea. (There were tea-shops in plenty at Didford, but she had already been at the expense of lunch while awaiting the trial, and two meals out in one day simply did not enter into Mrs. Pink's scheme of things.) A heavily built woman, she shifted her weight uneasily from one foot to the other as she watched the hands of the town clock creep slowly towards the hour.

It still wanted ten minutes to four when release came unexpectedly in the shape of a very dirty jeep, which pulled up, clattering and quivering, opposite the bus-stop. Above the noise of the engine she heard Horace Wendon's voice saying, "Can I give you a lift back to Yewbury, Mrs. Pink?"

Wendon was in a comparatively cheerful mood. He had spent

the better part of a month's instalment on his judgment debt lunching in Didford, and capped that extravagance with an orgy of buying at a farm sale nearby. Farm sales were to him what the bottle is to other unsuccessful men, and almost as ruinous. He could not resist the fascinating assortment of oddments that these functions always produce. His smallholding was already littered with objects that he had bought in the past because they were going cheap, and the jeep was now overflowing with fresh acquisitions which, in the teeth of past experience, he yet firmly believed would come in handy one day.

He cleared a roll of rotten wire netting off the seat beside him to make room for his passenger. Mrs. Pink climbed gratefully in, and they shot erratically down the High Street.

"I saw you in court this morning, didn't I?" he said, when they were at last free of the traffic and out on the main road. "What was your trouble? Mine was bad pig meal, as I expect you heard."

"Mr. Todman took me to court," Mrs. Pink explained. "He wants my cottage back for his Marlene to live in."

Mr. Wendon was genuinely concerned. "That's a bad business," he said. "Where will you go? Yewbury can't get along without you, you know."

"The judge said I could stay. It seems that Marlene being only a stepdaughter made all the difference. I don't understand it really, and no more did Mr. Todman. He was ever so upset."

Horace Wendon seldom laughed, and then usually at the expense of others. He did so now.

"I bet he was!" he said. "That will make him really mad. Serve him right, the old robber!"

"I wouldn't say that, Mr. Wendon," said Mrs. Pink gently. "Marlene really does want the cottage. I'd be glad to go if I could."

"You hold on to what you can," replied Wendon. "It's no good being too generous in this world. Todman can find somewhere else for the girl if he wants to. He's rich enough, to judge

24

by what he charged me for overhauling this contraption. And now," he relapsed into his usual depression, "I suppose he'll start pressing me for his bill."

Nothing more was said between them until he deposited Mrs. Pink at the door of the disputed cottage.

"I'm sure I'm very grateful to you, Mr. Wendon," she said as she got out. "Would you care to come in for a cup of tea?"

There was a shade of diffidence in the giving of the invitation that marked her recognition of the fact that, in spite of everything, Mr. Wendon was still hanging on to the skirts of the gentry, and might regard it as a liberty. Wendon, whose misfortunes had aggravated his class-consciousness, hesitated before he accepted. He did so, he told himself, because he did not wish to offend her. All the same, it was odd finding himself the casual guest of a village woman! He had the feeling as he entered her door that he was in some obscure way crossing the Rubicon.

"If you'll just sit there a minute while I boil the kettle…" said Mrs. Pink and disappeared into the kitchen.

Wendon looked around him in some surprise. The room was much better furnished than he had expected. It was grotesquely overcrowded, of course, but some of the pieces were quite good. The desk in the corner, laden with neatly arranged papers, was a solid mahogany affair which his own father would not have been ashamed of owning. There were even some quite respectable pictures on the walls….

He was examining one of these when Mrs. Pink returned with the tea. It was a *Vanity Fair* cartoon by "Spy", depicting an elderly man with a bushy white beard and prodigious frontal development, a dripping quill pen in his hand.

"That's an interesting thing you have there," he said. "I've seen one like it before, somewhere. It's of Henry Spicer, isn't it?"

"I don't know, I'm sure," said Mrs. Pink vaguely.

"Henry Spicer," Wendon persisted. "The writer at Yew Hill people used to make such a fuss about." Then, seeing that Mrs. Pink still looked blank, he added, "How did you come by it?"

"It was something my husband had, like all the rest," she said shortly. "Do you take sugar in your tea, Mr. Wendon?"

"Yes, please. There's something written in the corner. Such a scribble I can't make it out. 'Yours truly...' By Jove! It's an autograph. You know, Mrs. Pink, this might be worth quite a bit of money. If it was mine I'd sell it."

"Oh, I couldn't do that. Won't you sit down and have your tea, Mr. Wendon?"

Though he was not particularly quick on the uptake, Wendon realized that his hostess was not prepared to discuss the picture. He sat down, and the tea was consumed for the most part in silence. As soon as he decently could, he rose to go.

"Sorry to rush away," he observed, "but I've got a little business I promised to do for Mrs. Ransome up at The Alps." He took another look at the "Spy" cartoon as he went. "Ugly old blighter," he observed. "He puts me in mind of something, but I can't think what. I still think you ought to sell him for what he can fetch."

Mrs. Pink did not attempt to keep him. Her hospitality had already delayed her from something else more important in her eyes even than tea. When he had gone she did not even wait to wash up the tea things. Instead she put on once more her battered black straw hat, walked out of her house, down the lane past the Huntsman's Inn, across the road and through the lych-gate of the churchyard just opposite.

It was cool and dim inside the church. The garish stained-glass windows with which pious nineteenth-century restorers had ornamented the Norman building let in little of the faint spring sunshine. Mrs. Pink stood for a moment at the west end while her eyes grew accustomed to the half-light, and the peace that the church had never yet failed to bring descended upon her. She noticed that electric lights were burning beyond the choir-screen, to the north of the altar. That would be in the Harvill Chapel. Visitors were always coming to see the monu-

26

ments there. Mrs. Pink, who loved the church, stained glass and all, with uncritical adoration, cared less for the Harvill Chapel than for any other part of it. It was more like a museum than a place of worship, she thought, with its rows of stiffly sculptured squires and ladies lying on their tombs, and even piled one above another against the wall, for all the world like passengers in a third-class sleeping carriage on the railway. She let her eyes travel round the church. It was time to be thinking about flowers for Easter. She must remember to remind Lady Furlong to bring hers in good time this year. Last Easter they had not arrived till almost everything had been arranged, and it had been most awkward persuading Mrs. Blenkiron to take her arms off the altar to make room for her ladyship's eucharis.... Guiltily, Mrs. Pink told herself that this was not the object for which she was in the church that afternoon. She recalled her wandering thoughts, slipped into a pew and knelt down in prayer. She remained on her knees for a long time.

When she finally rose to her feet, her headache now gone, and even her craving for tea temporarily forgotten, she observed that the light was still on in the Harvill Chapel. Visitors did not often stay there as long as this. One dead Harvill looked much like another and their curiosity was usually quickly satisfied. Possibly they had gone and forgotten to turn off the lights. If, on the other hand, they were still there they were being remarkably quiet for tourists, which probably meant that they were Up To No Good. In either case, it was her clear duty to take action.

Mrs. Pink walked quietly up the length of the church. Turning to her left just past the choir-screen, she entered the chapel. At first she thought that it was empty. Then, peering over a high, late Renaissance tomb, she saw a figure kneeling on the floor just beneath the north window. The carpet had been rolled back, and he was vigorously scrubbing away with a short black stick at a long sheet of paper, kept in place by piles of hassocks and hymn-books at the corners.

The effigy of Sir Guy d'Harville has a modest celebrity among connoisseurs of English brasses as a sound, if not outstanding, specimen of early fifteenth-century work. Mrs. Pink was aware of its existence, though she had never troubled to examine it. She could see that something unusual was going on in its vicinity, and her immediate conclusion was that the intruder was indeed Up To No Good. She advanced firmly upon him and said, as loudly as her respect for her surroundings would allow, "What are you doing here?"

The stranger stood up, and Mrs. Pink realized with relief that she had to do with a boy, not more than seventeen years old. He was tall for his age, thin and spectacled, and appeared perfectly self-possessed.

"Good afternoon," he said politely. "I heard you, but I thought it was the verger coming to lock up. I've been taking a rubbing of the brass."

"Nobody's allowed to take anything out of the church without permission," said Mrs. Pink severely.

The boy looked pained.

"Naturally I've got permission," he said. "I asked the Vicar on Sunday. He told me I could come any time the church wasn't being used. And I'm not taking anything from the church, actually. Only an impression of the brass. It's like taking a photograph, really, only much better. I'm just about finished now. Would you like to look at it?"

He stood away from the sheet of paper and proudly exhibited the results of his labours. Mrs. Pink looked down uncomprehendingly at Sir Guy's mailed figure, severe in black and white.

"It's very ugly," she observed.

"It's a jolly good impression," the boy protested. "The skirt of taces is a bit blurred, perhaps, but the brass is rather badly worn there, anyway. The gorget is a great success. I thought it would be a bit tricky." He returned the hassocks and hymn-books to their proper places, pocketed his black stick and rolled up the strip of paper.

"What are you going to do with it?" Mrs. Pink asked.

"I shall hang it up in my room, naturally. I've got quite a decent collection already. Last holidays I was able to get Stoke b'Aberon." He breathed the name with reverence. "There's nothing so good as that in Markshire, of course, but according to Boutell there are two fairly interesting ones at Didford Magna. I shall try them next week." He rolled the carpet back over Sir Guy. "I'm afraid I'm boring you," he added politely.

Mrs. Pink did not contradict him, but she was looking at him with interest.

"I saw you in church last Sunday, didn't I?" she said. "Are you staying in these parts?"

"Well, actually I suppose I should say I'm living here, when I'm not at school. At least, I imagine I shall be living here from now on. I'm at The Alps."

"You'll be young Mr. Ransome, then?"

"My fame has evidently preceded me," said the boy gravely. "Yes, I'm Godfrey Ransome."

"I was wondering," said Mrs. Pink hesitantly. "That is, the Vicar was asking me—do you think Mrs. Ransome would care to help with the refreshments at the summer bazaar? I didn't like to trouble her, but perhaps you could enquire?"

"I could ask if you like, of course. Unfortunately, I don't know my mother very well, but I should rather doubt if it was in her line. However, there is no harm in trying."

He prepared to leave the chapel. Mrs. Pink came with him.

"I've never heard a lad of your age say he doesn't know his own mother," she said in shocked tones, as they reached the choir. "It doesn't sound natural to me."

"Mine has been a somewhat unusual childhood," he replied shortly. "By the way, I notice there are six candlesticks on the altar. Did your vicar get a faculty for them?"

"I couldn't say, I'm sure."

"I was only asking because one of the boys at school has a father who's chancellor to a diocese. He's awfully down on that sort of thing. Personally, I couldn't care less."

They parted at the door of the church. Mrs. Pink left Godfrey attaching his rubbing to the back of a rather battered bicycle and made her way home. She washed up the tea, carefully swept up the crumbs which Mr. Wendon had left on the carpet as a memento of his visit, and then sat down at her desk and opened her typewriter. There was much to do. First she dealt with Colonel Sampson's almost illegible agenda for the forthcoming meeting of the British Legion. Next she composed several appeals to laggard subscribers to the Friends of Yew Hill. She was about to turn her attention to the affairs of the Moral Welfare Association, when there was a knock at the front door, which was also the door into the sitting-room.

Mr. Todman stood on the threshold, his yellow hair standing up in the evening breeze, his hard little face pale and determined.

"Come in, Mr. Todman," said Mrs. Pink gently. "Won't you sit down?"

Mr. Todman would not sit down. He stood in the middle of the little room and came to business at once.

"Mrs. Pink," he said, "will you take three hundred pounds?"

"For what, Mr. Todman?"

"For this shack, Mrs. Pink. It's more than what my dad gave for it."

"It's less than I could get any other place for, Mr. Todman, the price things are now. You know that."

"Maybe it is, Mrs. Pink, but this happens to be my house. You're forgetting that. I'm offering you three hundred, just to get out."

"I couldn't do it, Mr. Todman."

"I tell you what, Mrs. Pink. You can have the room over the garage what Marlene's got now—*and* three hundred. That's a fair offer, ain't it?"

"I'm not saying it isn't, Mr. Todman. But it wouldn't do, you know it wouldn't. I'd like to help Marlene if I could, but I must have a place to myself. It's worth more to me than money. That's what I told the judge."

"Judge, my foot!" Mr. Todman was so agitated that he departed for once from the civil Yewbury custom of repeating the name of the person he was addressing. "What did he know about it? Why, he wasn't so much as a proper judge at that, but a silly old man they'd dug out of a ditch to sit there and keep people out of their rights!"

"I can't help that, Mr. Todman. If the law says I can stay here, then I shall just stay, till I can find some place else."

"And when will that be, may I ask?"

"I cannot say, Mr. Todman. Quite soon, perhaps. Perhaps not." Mr. Todman shifted his line of attack.

"You told a lot of lies in court this afternoon," he said.

Mrs. Pink was startled out of the tranquillity which she had maintained up to that moment.

"Mr. Todman, what do you mean by that?" she cried, in a voice sharpened by fear.

Mr. Todman saw that his random shot had struck, but was clearly unable to press home his advantage.

"A lot of lies," he repeated. "I heard them, and so did a heap of other people. You'd best be careful, I'm telling you, Mrs. Pink."

"I swore on the Book that I'd tell the truth," said Mrs. Pink firmly. "And if I said one word that was wrong"—she looked round her for a moment, hesitated, and then went on defiantly—"may God strike me where I sit!"

Mr. Todman was impressed in spite of himself. He looked hopefully at her to see whether her challenge would be accepted, and then, seeing his opponent still in her chair and apparently none the worse, moved slowly to the door. But he still had one more word to say.

"I'm going now," he said. "But mark my words, Mrs. Pink. I shall have my Marlene in this place one way or another before you're much older—law or no law. I'm warning you."

"Over my dead body, Mr. Todman!"

"If you like it that way, Mrs. Pink!"

The door slammed behind him.

Mrs. Pink turned back to her desk and inserted a new sheet of paper in her typewriter. But it was some time before she could collect herself sufficiently to resume her work. "A lot of lies!" she repeated to herself. Nobody had ever dared suggest such a thing of her before. And now...But she hadn't lied—not what anybody could call lying. She had explained it all to God that afternoon in church, and He had assured her that he understood. Her conscience was as clear as it had always been. But would Mr. Todman understand if he ever found out? Would that nice old gentleman who had looked at her so oddly and then told her she could stay in the cottage? Why had the Lord chosen to put so great a burden on His weak servant, Martha Pink? She looked at the calendar on the wall. It would not be for long now, please God.

She began to type a letter for the Moral Welfare Association, and forgot her troubles in the task. But they returned again when, her work for others completed, she had to attend to her own affairs. Among the pile of papers on her desk was a letter which had reached her that morning from a firm of London solicitors.

"Dear Madam [it ran],

We have received notice..."

She read and re-read the letter, shaking her head in dumb despair. The words and figures wavered before her tired eyes. Miserably, at last she braced herself to the task of composing a reply.

4

The Prodigal Mother

A narrow, winding lane runs off the main road past Henry Spicer's cottage. Thence it climbs the valley that divides the north face of Yew Hill in two, by a slope too steep for a bicycle ridden by any but the most athletic boy. Godfrey did not pretend to be particularly athletic. He dismounted at the first bend and wheeled Sir Guy d'Harville up the hill. He was in no great hurry and treated himself to a breather at the second bend. He was already late for tea, but his mother was not likely to make a fuss about that. As he had told Mrs. Pink, he did not know his mother very well; but in the last few days he had learned that whatever her shortcomings fussiness was not among them. That was certainly a point in her favour.

When one came to think of it, Godfrey told himself, letting his eye travel over the dark tops of the yews towards the vale of the Didder below, his mother had quite a number of good points—far more than one would have guessed from the hints which his father had dropped from time to time. In his methodical fashion he set himself to enumerate them. First and foremost, she was extremely attractive. Nobody, not even his father, had ever been able to deny that. Moreover, she was intelligent. It was a pity, he reflected coolly, that she had never been taught to apply her intelligence properly, but for all that she was no fool. Finally, she was undoubtedly good-natured. That was the most important point of all, and affected more significant things than whether or not he was expected to be home punctually for tea. It was not everything, of course, but it was enough to go on with. On the whole, there was no reason why the Easter holidays should not be a success. At all events, the experiment should prove interesting. He picked up his bicycle and resumed the climb.

Marian Ransome, at that moment, was sitting placidly in her drawing-room, smoking a cigarette and contemplating a glass of sherry. She was thinking about Godfrey, but, as he had justly estimated, she was not fussing about him. In a highly variegated career, she had seldom made a fuss about anything. When her marriage to Professor Ransome had proved a lamentable failure she had quietly abandoned him in favour of one of his junior colleagues at the university. The ensuing fuss, which was considerable, she had left to be made by others. If she had regretted leaving her two-year-old son behind, she had not said so. The ups and downs of the next fifteen years had in no way impaired her equanimity; and when, on the Professor's sudden death, Godfrey had been inspired to propose himself as her guest for the holidays, she had, as always, been ready to accept the offer of a new experience. Up to now, she had not regretted it, deriving a certain bewildered satisfaction from observing what a severely academic upbringing could do to her own flesh and blood.

Her glass was nearly finished when her son finally appeared.

"Well, Godfrey," she said in her lazy, purring voice, "you look as if a glass of sherry would do you good. Tea's been done and cleared away long ago."

"Actually, I don't care for sherry very much," said Godfrey. "I'll ask Grethe to make me another pot."

"Well, you'll be careful, won't you? You know how temperamental these Austrians are. She'll give notice as soon as look at you."

"That will be quite all right," said Godfrey confidently. "I shall tell her a funny story in German and she'll do anything."

He was away some time before he returned with a laden tray. Mrs. Ransome looked at it enviously.

"She told me there were none of those cream-cakes left," she observed. "I suppose she was keeping them for herself. Was it a very funny story, Godfrey?"

"She seemed to be amused by it. She told me two of her own back. One of them"—he frowned as he attacked the cakes—"was not very proper."

"My poor Godfrey, that must have been painful for you. But what a lot I miss by not knowing German! You'll have to teach me some day. Don't spoil your appetite for dinner. That nice little Mr. Wendon dropped in just now with a joint of pork. Grethe is going to do something very continental with it."

"If that nice little Mr. Wendon goes in for illicit pig-killing, Mother, do you really think you ought to encourage him?"

Mrs. Ransome opened her fine eyes wide in surprise. "Good gracious!" she exclaimed. "Do they teach you that sort of thing at school? I thought it was all Greek and Latin and so on."

"They don't teach us pig-killing, naturally," said Godfrey seriously. "But it's only common sense that when a man drops bits of pork at people's back doors he's liable to get into trouble."

"Well, I'm disappointed, that's all. I'd planned the pork as a pleasant little surprise for you, and now I suppose you'll refuse to eat it on principle——"

"I never said I wouldn't eat it, Mother, I was only pointing out——"

"—though I should hardly have thought that taking a bit of meat that was going begging was any worse than worming cream-cakes out of Grethe by telling her dirty stories."

"Really, Mother! I——" Godfrey looked up to find that his mother was laughing at him. He stopped abruptly, looking and feeling rather sheepish.

"I'm sorry, Godfrey," Mrs. Ransome said kindly. "You mustn't mind my pulling your leg now and then. So far as the pork goes, I know it was very wicked of me, but I am a wicked woman, and you'll have to get used to it. I felt so sorry for poor Mr. Wendon. A horrible judge has just told him that he has to pay a lot of money he doesn't really owe, and we can't blame him for trying to make it up somehow. It isn't as if he was an ordinary pigman, anyway. He was at your school."

"He was at Harrow," said Godfrey loftily.

"Well, it's the same thing, isn't it? I mean, it's just as good.... No, Godfrey, don't jump down my throat. I ought to have remembered there are some things too sacred to make jokes about. Now tell me about your doings this afternoon. Was the brass-rubbing a success?"

"Quite successful. Would you like to look at it?"

Mrs. Ransome shook her head. "Better not," she said. "I should only annoy you by saying the wrong thing, and I've plagued you enough for one day. You can show it to Grethe, if you like. Perhaps she would find something improper to say about it."

"I met someone while I was in the church—a Mrs. Pink."

"Mrs. Pink? Yes, I know her—poor, dear Mrs. Pink."

"I thought she was rather nice."

"So she is. The very pink of perfection. Altogether too good for me, I'm afraid. Did she try to sell you a raffle ticket in aid of the church roof or something?"

"Not exactly. But she did mention the midsummer bazaar. The Vicar wants to know if you would help with the refreshments."

"The Vicar must be in his dotage! I never heard such nonsense. Seriously, Godfrey, can you imagine me selling lemonade at a Church bazaar?"

"I don't see why not," said Godfrey gallantly. "I'm sure you'd look jolly nice."

"Of course I should look jolly nice, as you put it. And all the ladies of Yewbury, who will certainly look jolly awful, would have a fit at the sight of me. Because I am not respectable, Godfrey, do get that into your head. I am not fit to associate with Lady Furlong and Mrs. So Long and all the rest of them. Surely your father must have mentioned it to you at some time or another?"

"Well—yes," said Godfrey, pink with embarrassment, "I suppose, in a sort of a way, he did."

"Very well. Then don't try to pretend facts aren't there because they're uncomfortable, which was a weakness of your father's, who was remarkably like you in some ways, and much too good for me," said Mrs. Ransome breathlessly. "Now I'm going upstairs to lie down before dinner, which is another thing no respectable woman does nowadays. Here's something to amuse you meanwhile—the *Times Literary Supplement*. The boy must have delivered it by mistake."

"As a matter of fact I ordered it," said Godfrey. "I hope you don't mind."

"Mind? Of course not, so long as you don't want to read me any of it aloud. It will be quite like old times. I haven't seen the dreary old rag for years."

She kissed her son affectionately on the top of his head and vanished.

"By the way," said Mrs. Ransome some time later in the evening. "I've asked a friend to stay. I ought to have mentioned it sooner. Are you sure it won't upset your plans?"

"Why should it?" said Godfrey, who after an excellent meal of illicit pork was feeling at peace with the world.

"Oh, I don't know. I just thought it might, that was all."

"Is it a male or female friend?"

"Male, of course. I haven't any female friends—surely you've gathered that by now. You're not shocked?"

"My dear mother, I hope I am sufficiently broad-minded——"

Mrs. Ransome giggled uncontrollably. The boy was really ludicrously like his father. Then she became serious again. "His name is Rose," she said deliberately, "Humphrey Rose."

"Yes?"

"You haven't heard of him?"

"I can't say that I have. Ought I to know the name?"

Mrs. Ransome looked relieved at his ignorance.

"Oh well, it was a long time ago—you must have been quite small. But he was rather—celebrated once. I hope you'll like him."

"I'm sure I shall." There was something about his mother's manner that brought a little doubt into Godfrey's voice. "When does he arrive?"

"I'm not quite certain when he will be—at liberty to come. Possibly tomorrow. In a day or two, anyway. I don't suppose he will bother you much. He's really coming for a rest."

They talked of other things, and shortly afterwards Godfrey went up to his room. Before undressing he removed one of his mother's favourite watercolours from the wall and pinned Sir Guy d'Harville up in its place. In bed, he lay awake for some time reading the *Times Literary Supplement*. It is the charm of that periodical that the reader never knows from column to column what aspect of learning he will encounter next. Godfrey, with the omnivorous gusto of his age, read successively a leading article on Nineteenth-century Nonconformism, a severe review of a restatement of Ricardo's Theory of Rent and an appreciative notice of a new edition of Higden's *Polychronicon*. Thence he turned to lighter fare—a group of books of reminiscence reviewed together. He was already half asleep when a name that he had heard recently caught his eye. Jerking himself awake, he read the sentence once more:

"Among much that is of minor interest, Sir John adds a valuable footnote to contemporary history when he reveals the part played by the future Prime Minister in exposing the scandal which brought the career of Humphrey Rose, M.P., to an abrupt and shameful conclusion."

The reviewer did not explain further. Obviously the affair of Humphrey Rose was the sort of thing one was supposed to know about without being told—like so many other things, thought Godfrey resentfully. But he had said enough. This man Rose—his mother's intended visitor—was a ruffian. Godfrey's imagination, always active, conjured up half a dozen lurid crimes of which his proposed fellow guest might have been guilty. Really, he told himself, he was fairly broad-minded, but there were limits! He must speak to his mother very seriously in the morning.

He switched off the light and was asleep at once.

5

Humphrey Rose

Judge Jefferson was still a sick man, and his deputy continued to be called upon to fill his place. Pettigrew travelled the length and breadth of Markshire. He passed from draughty town halls, where inaudible witnesses competed vainly with the roar of traffic outside, to stuffy police-courts loud with the clamour of imprisoned stray dogs. Daily he was called upon to solve the insoluble, to divine the truth between competing perjuries, to apportion derisory incomes among innumerable creditors, or to discover what had caused two stationary cars, each hugging its proper side of the road, to smash each other to pieces in the middle of the highway. He found time in the intervals to order the adoption of dozens of babies. He enjoyed himself immensely.

The last sitting before the Easter vacation was at Markhampton. Pettigrew occupied the old Assize Court there, recalling battles long ago on the Southern Circuit, while he listened to a long and preternaturally dull dispute relating to a dressmaker's bill. (In his innocence, he did not realize that anything relating to women's clothes is automatically News, and he was astonished to find the case featured in all but one of the next morning's newspapers, garnished with a quantity of judicial sallies which he was quite unconscious of having uttered.) He finished the case eventually in time to catch one of the few trains that amble from Markhampton along the branch line following the valley of the Didder. A moment after he had taken his seat the express from London thundered into the station on the other side of the platform. Looking from the window, Pettigrew casually observed a middle-aged man leave a first-class carriage opposite. The passenger waited patiently until he had attracted the attention of a porter, to whom he handed a very small suitcase, apparently all the luggage he had. Followed by the porter, he then strolled jauntily across the width of the platform, entered Pettigrew's compartment, sat down in the corner opposite and rewarded the porter for his labour with a half-crown. It was difficult to say which of the two men seemed the more pleased with the transaction.

A moment later the train started. The newcomer produced a large cigar, which he began to smoke with almost exaggerated enjoyment. Pettigrew looked at him with interest—an interest not untinged with envy. He had seldom seen anybody of mature years so completely happy as was this stranger. It seemed unnatural that a man in this age and hemisphere could be quite so pleased with himself and with his surroundings. He looked out of the window at the passing suburbs of Markhampton and beamed with joy as though they had been the most beautiful buildings on earth. He looked round the sordid compartment with its dirty paint-work and fly-blown advertisements of remote beauty-spots, and even that seemed to meet with his ecstatic approval. It was quite heartening merely to look at him. Best of all, from Pettigrew's point of view, he was satisfied to admire the world and all that was therein in silence. The fact that he made no attempt to extend his pleasure in life by addressing a word to his fellow passenger contradicted Pettigrew's first impression that here was merely an American visitor, enjoying the peculiarities of a foreign scene, and not yet familiar with the normal tariff of English porters.

41

The odd thing is, Pettigrew told himself, I'm sure I've seen this fellow before, but I can't for the life of me think where. He studied him closely over the top of his evening paper. He saw a short, full-featured man, neatly dressed in a suit that hung rather loosely upon him. His eyes were very bright, his expression full of vitality, but in marked contrast to this his cheeks were flabby and his complexion was noticeably pale. An unhealthy pallor, Pettigrew thought. It put him in mind of—of what, exactly? His brain was tired after his day in court, and again the connection eluded him. He dozed as the train pottered on down the valley.

When Pettigrew alighted at his station his companion followed him out of the train, and again waited for a porter to take his bag. At the station entrance Pettigrew saw Mr. Todman, sitting at the wheel of the high, old-fashioned saloon which was Yewbury's state chariot for weddings, funerals and distinguished visitors. Unashamedly inquisitive, he loitered outside, and was rewarded in due course by the appearance of the stranger.

"Are you the gentleman for The Alps, sir?" asked Mr. Todman.

"The Alps it is," was the reply, in a rich, creamy baritone.

Some voices are more memorable than the faces that go with them. It only needed those four syllables for Pettigrew to remember exactly who the speaker was and where and how he had last seen him.

"Well, I'll be blowed!" he murmured as the hired car drove away. Exactly the same remark was being made at the same moment by the porter as he contemplated the largesse in his hand.

"We have acquired an interesting new neighbour," said Pettigrew to his wife that evening. "Humphrey Rose is staying at The Alps."

"Rose? I thought he went to prison."

"He did—for seven years. The Family Fundholdings swindle.

He can only be just out. Prison life didn't suit him, to judge by his looks. I had the pleasure of his company in the train."

"What is he like?"

Pettigrew wrinkled his nose in thought before he gave his opinion.

"A callous, selfish brute," he said finally. "He brings destruction and misery wherever he goes. A man of extraordinary charm, generous and kind-hearted."

"Well?" said Eleanor. "Which is he? He can't be both."

"Indeed he can. That's what makes him so dangerous."

On second thoughts, Godfrey had decided to postpone his serious talk to his mother about the impending visitor. He was not in the least afraid of her, but he had a strong objection to being laughed at, and laughter would, he felt, be the only response that he was likely to get to any protest. The proper course, he decided, would be to register his disapproval by a cold and dignified attitude towards the unwanted guest. The contrast between his own impeccable behaviour and the orgies in which a man of bad character would be certain to indulge—Godfrey was a little vague on this point, but orgies, he thought, there were certain to be—would tell its own tale. His mother, after all, knew the difference between right and wrong—witness her evident appreciation of Mrs. Pink—and it was his duty as a son to help her to choose the right way. If the worse came to the worst, and he failed in his attempt, he would abandon the contaminated house and finish his holidays somewhere on his own.

On the evening of Rose's arrival, therefore, Godfrey immured himself with his books and brass-rubbings until dinner-time. It would be time enough to greet the visitor when he had to. He was aware of the sound of a warm, resonant and—he was bound to admit—cultured voice downstairs, but he firmly shut his ears to any distractions. When the moment came he went down to the drawing-room with a carefully arranged expression of blended civility and distaste.

"Humphrey, this is my son Godfrey," said Mrs. Ransome as he entered.

Rose was sitting in a deep armchair on the farther side of the room. The words were hardly out of her mouth before he fairly leaped to his feet and strode across the intervening space with extended hand.

"I'm delighted to meet you, sir," he said. "Delighted."

Astonishingly, he really did seem delighted. Godfrey's intention had been merely to bow distantly, but somehow his hand, too, had come out automatically and he found it being warmly shaken.

"You are at school, I take it?" said Rose with eager interest. "Where is that?"

Godfrey told him.

"A scholar, of course? But I needn't ask. I could see that as soon as you came into the room. My congratulations! You are greatly privileged. What are you reading? Classics? Languages?"

Again, Godfrey could not but oblige with the information. It struck him as he did so that his mother, for all her charm, had never been in the least impressed by his scholastic attainments, nor even asked what his special subjects at school were.

"You'll be going up to the university later, no doubt," Rose was saying. "To your father's college, I hope. I remember meeting him once. He impressed me tremendously. You know, Marian,"—he turned to Mrs. Ransome—"you made a terrible mistake when you parted company with your husband."

"My dear Humphrey! That from you, of all people!"

"I am perfectly serious. The break-up of families through divorce is one of the greatest evils of the day. I am sure your son will agree with me."

Godfrey's head began to spin. So far from indulging in orgies, the scandalous Mr. Rose had not even finished his glass of sherry, and now was taking his side against his mother in the interests of morality. Could the *Times Literary Supplement* have got its facts right?

44

"But I was talking about the university," Rose went on. "I don't know if you've decided on your career yet, but an academic life—if you're fitted for it—must be the finest thing in the world. I went to work when I was fourteen, and I've never ceased to regret it. What do I know of the things that really matter? I had to waste my time in business—politics—rubbish of that kind. I've picked up a few scraps of learning here and there since, but it's not the same thing. That's one reason why I'm always glad to meet someone who's had the luck to be properly educated. There are a lot of things I'd like your opinion about...."

And indeed throughout dinner and after Rose continued not only to talk agreeably and amusingly but also to listen with flattering deference to any views that Godfrey was pleased to express. He examined with absorbed interest the rubbing of Sir Guy d'Harville and, unlike Mrs. Ransome, found exactly the right thing to say. He told some good stories about famous political figures, and, more important, laughed generously when Godfrey ventured on an anecdote of his own. Long before the evening was over Godfrey had completely forgotten that this was the man about whom he had intended to speak seriously to his mother. He found it impossible to resist Rose. Indeed the contest was over almost before it had begun. The charm that in the past had wheedled thousands of pounds from hard-headed men of business was now turned with full force upon a schoolboy, and the schoolboy inevitably surrendered.

The enchanted evening ended too soon for Godfrey. Rose professed himself to be tired and wished to go to bed early. Before doing so, however, he insisted on taking a turn on the terrace outside the french windows of the drawing-room. Godfrey accompanied him. The air was keen, and a bright moon bathed in light the yews at the head of the Druids' Glade, stretching down the hill into the mists of the valley below. A bat flew gibbering low over their heads.

"'Wanton wheels the bat's wing round my cottage dwelling',"

quoted Rose unexpectedly. "'Something as the something'—how does it go? Ah, I remember:

"'Fickle as the loved one that calls and bids me go'." He chanted the rest of the stanza. "You know the *Yew Hill Eclogues*, of course. What do young men of today think of Henry Spicer?"

"One reads his poetry, some of it," Godfrey told him. "The novels, of course, are quite unreadable nowadays. The style—".

A violent sneeze cut short his pontifications.

"My dear fellow, you're catching cold! How very selfish of me to bring you out on a night like this!" He hastily led the way indoors. "You know," he went on, as he drew the curtains of the window behind them, "I hesitate to suggest it, but I think the young men of today are wrong about Henry Spicer. He was a most remarkable fellow, and once you get used to his mannerisms the novels are very enjoyable. I've read *The Solipsist* three times, and the third reading was the best. You should try it. It takes an intelligent person like you to appreciate it. I met Spicer once when I was about your age, by the way, and he——But it's too late to embark on another story. It must wait till tomorrow."

"I suppose you read his books because you'd met him," said Mrs. Ransome. "Otherwise I can't imagine that stuff like that would be in your line."

"Oh no," said Rose simply. "I only took to reading them because they happened to be in the prison library. Good night."

"Godfrey," said Mrs. Ransome as she kissed her son good night, "I feel that I ought to warn you about Humphrey Rose. He's not always like this by any manner of means. You will be careful with him, won't you?"

And that, thought Godfrey as he made his way up to bed, was positively the last straw.

6

The Acquaintances
of Mr. Rose

Godfrey was late down to breakfast next morning. He was not
sorry to find that Mr. Rose had been an earlier riser and was
even then pacing the lawn outside with all the enjoyment that
might have been expected from a man to whom such an exercise
had been long denied. He took the opportunity to ask his mother, in suitably reproachful tones, precisely for what offence her
guest had been imprisoned. Mrs. Ransome, however, was disap-
pointingly vague. It was, she said, something to do with money.
Her manner suggested that a mere peccadillo of that kind
should not be taken too seriously.

"Your money is in trust until you're twenty-one, I suppose?"
she added. "You ought to be quite safe with Humphrey, then. All
the same, I shouldn't sign anything if he should happen to want
you to." She concluded by proposing that if Godfrey was really
curious about Rose's misdeeds he should ask him himself—a
suggestion that Godfrey turned down with some annoyance.

He was finishing his breakfast in a somewhat uncertain frame
of mind when the rattle of a badly sprung vehicle outside
brought Mrs. Ransome to her feet.

"Thank goodness, there's Mr. Wendon!" she exclaimed. "Catering just before Easter is such a problem, and I was beginning to wonder——No, Godfrey, it's quite all right this time—simply two perfectly legitimate chickens."

She went to the door, and Godfrey followed her. He was able to satisfy himself that this time the transaction was perfectly legal. The fowls were handed over, weighed, and paid for, and Wendon was just getting back into his jeep when Rose strolled up across the lawn. The fresh air had put some colour into his cheeks, his eyes shone with the pleasure of living, and he walked with the spring of a man without a care in the world.

"Good morning," he called to Godfrey. "I hope you didn't catch cold last night. Ah, Wendon, my dear fellow, I'm delighted to see you again."

Wendon did not say anything for an appreciable time. His pale face had gone a shade paler, he was breathing very hard, and he was staring at the visitor with set and angry eyes.

"What the hell are *you* doing here?" he said at last.

"I'm staying in these parts for a few days," said Rose easily. "And how is the world treating you?"

Wendon left the jeep and walked across the drive to where Rose was standing. He stopped no more than a foot or two away and thrust his head forward till their faces almost touched.

"You double-crossing little twister!" he said. "How do you expect the world to be treating me, as you put it? You bleed a man white—leave him to whistle for his money—and then sail in, as cool as a cucumber, and ask a question like that!"

Wendon had a highly interested audience to his harangue. Grethe was leaning out of the kitchen window, a parcel of chicken giblets in her hand, drinking in every word. Mrs. Ransome, startled out of her usual serenity, clutched her son convulsively by the arm. Godfrey was wondering whether it was his duty to intervene before blood was shed, while at the same time he tried to keep count of Wendon's astonishing sequence of metaphors. Of them all, Rose was by far the least perturbed.

48

"You know, Wendon," he said in quiet, conversational tones, "I wonder whether you are being altogether fair. I told you at the time that there was an element of risk in the venture. You can't say I wasn't perfectly frank with you. And there was no reason why it shouldn't have come off, either. The trouble with you and the rest of them was being in too great a hurry. You pushed and prodded and burst the whole thing wide open, and there we were. And where I've been has been none too comfortable, I can assure you," he added with a disarming smile.

"And where," roared Wendon, "is my money?"

Rose shrugged his shoulders and shook his head with a gesture of sincere regret. He might have been a distinguished physician lamenting an incurable case.

"A fat lot you care!" cried Wendon. "We can all starve, while you're living in comfort on a woman!"

"Really, Mr. Wendon!" Mrs. Ransome intervened. "I think it is time you took yourself off. Mr. Rose may not mind being insulted in this way, but I do."

"You must excuse him, Marian," said Rose. "Mr. Wendon is, of course, justified to some extent in what he says, but not exactly in the sense that you understood. I am sure you did not intend any rudeness towards Mrs. Ransome, did you, Wendon? I do live—I always have lived—on other men—and women. After all, one must live on something. Mr. Wendon lives on pigs and poultry, I understand. I'm sure it's a much more satisfactory way of getting a living."

It was clear that by now the crisis was over. Under the equable flow of Rose's beautifully modulated voice Wendon's rage had subsided to angry mutterings. He was stalking back to the jeep when Rose's last words caught his ear.

"Satisfactory living!" he echoed. "I don't know what you call satisfactory, but it may interest you to know that I was put into the County Court last week for a debt of twenty-five pounds twelve and eightpence. That's the kind of satisfaction you've brought me down to!"

For the first time Rose showed real emotion. A look of distress passed across his face.

"My dear fellow!" he exclaimed. "My dear fellow!" He almost ran across to where Wendon, now at the wheel, was jabbing angrily at a recalcitrant self-starter. "I had no idea things were so bad. Really, this won't do at all! Put in the County Court for a petty debt—a man in your position—that's truly shocking!" A fat note-case had appeared in his hand. "How much did you say it was? Twenty-five pounds twelve and eight? You really must allow me...No, no, I insist. After all, it's only the merest trifle compared with what we so unfortunately lost together.... I'm afraid I haven't the precise sum here, but suppose we say thirty pounds?"

He pressed the notes into Wendon's hand. The latter looked at them incredulously.

"Well, I'll be damned!" he said.

His fist closed on the money and for a moment it looked as if he was about to fling it back into Rose's face. Then he changed his mind abruptly and thrust it into his pocket. Without saying another word, he jumped from his seat and swung furiously at the starting handle until the engine came to life with a roar. Then he climbed back into the seat, his face an angry brick red, his hands quivering. "Blast you!" he shouted above the noise of the engine. The jeep shot down the drive and out of the gate, scattering gravel as it went.

Mrs. Ransome was the first to break the silence that followed.

"You never told me that you knew Mr. Wendon, Humphrey," she said somewhat reproachfully.

"I wasn't expecting to meet him here, of course. But that's the worst of creditors. You never know where they'll turn up. I'm sorry for the disturbance, Marian."

"I'm sorry to think there may be no more chickens from Mr. Wendon. I've never seen a man in such a temper, and giving him that money only made it worse. You've wasted thirty pounds, I think."

50

"It was worth trying," said Rose, philosophically. "The reactions of these fellows are unpredictable. And he kept the money, which is a good sign."

"Thirty pounds!" Mrs. Ransome repeated. "It's a lot. Why do you carry so much cash about with you?"

"I have to. As an undischarged bankrupt I can't ask for credit without falling foul of the law. So what I want I must pay for on the nail. That's a tip worth remembering, young man," he added to Godfrey. "Beware of the man with his pockets full of money! The chances are that his cheques will all be stumers. Now in the days when I was solvent I often hadn't the price of a bus fare on me."

Godfrey, horribly embarrassed, found himself for once with nothing to say. He could not bring himself to ask the question that was uppermost in his mind. His mother, less inhibited, did it for him.

"And while you're giving good advice, Humphrey," she said, "perhaps you wouldn't mind telling us where the bankrupt gets all his cash to put in his pockets?"

Rose shrugged his shoulders.

"Well, you heard what our friend Wendon suggested just now," he said, shortly. "And now," he went on, changing the subject, "it's going to be a lovely day. I don't know about anyone else, but I should like a walk. In a day or two the hill is going to be crawling with Easter trippers. This should be our chance to enjoy it in comfort. What does anyone say?"

Walking, like church bazaars, was a recreation not in Mrs. Ransome's line. She accompanied Rose and Godfrey only as far as the first turning in the Druids' Glade, and then made her way back to the house.

From his study window Pettigrew saw the two ill-assorted figures emerge on to the green slope and make their way slowly down the hill. Rose chatted amiably as they went, and little by little the charm which he had laid on Godfrey the evening before began to reassert itself. But this time the process was slower and less complete. Against the background of wood and down, under the wide arc of the sky, Humphrey seemed to dwindle into something less important and far less interesting than he had seemed overnight in the close companionship of Mrs. Ransome's drawing-room. Godfrey even found himself yawning once or twice.

They found themselves in due course outside Henry Spicer's cottage. Rose's eyes brightened.

"Spicer!" he said. "I owe that man something!" He read the notice on the gate. "Spicer Memorial Museum. Entrance one shilling." "Shall we go in?"

The Spicer Museum, conceived at a time when the writer's reputation was at its height, is now little visited. They had the place to themselves save for a somnolent guardian. It had the slightly unreal air that a house once lived in and now a depository of miscellaneous relics always presents. Rose moved quickly from one exhibit to another, pausing only for a long, loving look at the manuscript of *The Solipsist* preserved in its glass case. He passed over the famous Whistler portrait with no more than a casual glance and came to rest finally before a Beerbohm caricature of the author in extreme old age.

"That's how I remember him," he said. "I told you I met him once, didn't I? I was in an accountant's office at the time, and he came in about his income-tax. It had gone up to something over a shilling in the pound, and he was fearfully worried. Of course tax evasion was in its infancy in those days. I was only a junior clerk—not more than an office-boy really, and it was no part of my job, but I was able to suggest something fairly useful and it made him very happy. I was very green, then, or I could have made something out of it for myself. As it was, I only got..."

He seemed to have forgotten Godfrey for the moment. "I wonder where that damned thing is now?" he murmured to himself. He stood abstractedly in the middle of the room, as though contemplating the green office-boy of those distant days and the long road that he had travelled since then. "Let's get out into the fresh air," he said abruptly. "It's musty in here."

Outside, Rose looked at the cottage with disfavour. "These museum people don't know their own business," he said. "Properly run, it should be worth a lot of money. It can't take enough to pay expenses as it is."

"Do you think a Spicer roadhouse would be better?" Godfrey suggested ironically. "With postcards and souvenirs on sale, and Solipsist teas at half a crown a head?"

"Why not?" said Rose. "Look what those Stratford fellows have done. Spicer isn't Shakespeare, but you could put him over just the same. It's simply a question of publicity. Publicity is the key to success, and why anyone should be afraid of it——"

"Good morning, Mr. Rose!" said a voice behind them. Rose swung round and found himself facing a young man with a camera. The shutter clicked, and the man jumped on to a bicycle and rode off towards the main road. Rose looked after him sourly.

"Now that will be in all tomorrow's papers, I suppose," he grumbled. "I shan't be able to stay here if that sort of thing goes on. I should have thought by now I was entitled to a certain amount of privacy if I wanted it."

"Perhaps Henry Spicer, too?" Godfrey suggested.

Rose had the grace to laugh. "Very well, we'll leave the museum as it is," he said. "But even by its own standards it's a poor show. I'd like to improve it if I could."

They strolled on down the lane to its junction with the road. The only traffic in view was a bicycle, travelling away from them in the direction of Yewbury. It was being ridden by a woman. She was in some difficulties up the moderately steep slope and wobbled dangerously from side to side. They were about to cross when a car shot past them, going in the same direction as the bicycle. It overtook it some fifty yards from where they stood. There was ample room for the car to pass, but instead of going over to its offside it appeared to drive directly at the labouring bicycle as it tottered on the crown of the road. At the last moment, when a collision seemed inevitable, the driver sounded his horn, at the same time swinging out by the barest minimum necessary to avoid running it down. The startled rider for her part made a vain attempt to get back to the side of the road, turned her handlebars too quickly and crashed to the ground, her machine on top of her, as the car dashed by.

"That," said Rose, "was a bloody piece of driving."

"He looked as if he was doing it on purpose," said Godfrey. "I wish I could have got his number."

"I didn't get it either, but it looked uncommonly like the hearse that met me at the station last night."

As they spoke they were hurrying to where the fallen bicyclist, having disentangled herself from her machine, was painfully trying to rise. Godfrey got to her first. It was not until he had his hands under her arms and was lifting her to her feet that he realized that he was clasping Mrs. Pink. He helped her to the side of the road, sat her down upon the bank and set himself rather clumsily to brush the dirt off her skirt with his hands. Rose, meanwhile, had picked up the bicycle and was salvaging the contents of the basket that lay strewn about the roadway.

It was clear that Mrs. Pink was not seriously hurt, but she was shocked and exhausted. She sat on the bank, her eyes closed, breathing heavily and clasping to her bosom the battered remains of her straw hat.

"We saw what happened," Godfrey told her. "It was a shocking bit of driving. We ought to tell the police. Did you get his number?"

"No, no," Mrs. Pink murmured faintly. "I don't want the police. I don't suppose Mr. Todman knew what he was doing. Marlene had her baby last night. I expect he's dreadfully upset."

"I think I've collected all your bits and pieces, madam," said Rose, wheeling the bicycle up to the bank.

At the sound of his voice Mrs. Pink opened her eyes.

"Humphrey," she said flatly.

54

"Well, if it isn't Martha!" said Rose.

And that, as Godfrey subsequently recorded with some surprise, was the only conversation that he heard exchanged between them.

Mrs. Pink stood up.

"I am feeling all right now," she answered. "I think I'd better be getting home."

Rose picked up the bicycle.

"Godfrey, my dear fellow," he said, "do you mind making my excuses to your mother and telling her that I shall not be back for lunch?"

Without another word said, Mrs. Pink set off along the road, walking slowly and stiffly. Rose went beside her, wheeling the bicycle. Whether they were talking as they went Godfrey could not determine. He watched them out of sight and then turned for home.

7

Postponement of a Bazaar

Two days of driving rain and mist had eliminated the view from
Pettigrew's window, and the dissertation on the Law of Torts
had profited accordingly. On the afternoon of Maundy Thursday
the weather miraculously improved, and Eleanor was not surprised on entering the study to find her husband unashamedly
occupied in looking out of the window. But this time she did not
share his enthusiasm.

"Have you read this week's *Didford Advertiser*, Frank?" she
asked, in a tone in which her husband's ear could detect a note
of reproach.

"Not yet," said Pettigrew. "I've been too busy since lunch. Do
look, Eleanor, there's a totally new effect since those beeches in
the foreground came out. It's quite remarkable how——"

But Eleanor refused to be sidetracked.

"You ought to," she said, and laid the paper on his desk.
"Lady Furlong's cook has given notice."

"Good heavens! I knew that her ladyship was a fairly important personage, but I had no idea that her domestic misfortunes
were hot news. Do let me see what it says."

"It doesn't say anything about the cook, naturally. Lady Furlong rang up just now to tell me. She's putting off our invitation to dinner next week."

"I'm sorry to hear that, but I don't quite see the connection."

"The cook has given notice because of something you said in the paper."

"Something *I* said? But, my dear girl, I've never written anything for the *Advertiser* in my life. And if I did it would certainly not be about my neighbour's cook. Cuckoos, perhaps—they are always a fair topic for correspondence at this time of the year. But not cooks. It's clean out of my line. There must be some mistake."

"There's no mistake at all. Just look at it yourself."

Pettigrew found himself confronted with yet another report of the dressmaker's action at Markhampton. The *Didford Advertiser's* layout did not run to the facetious headlines which had surprised him so much in the daily press. Instead, a column of solid print carried what he was horrified to see was an almost verbatim report of his judgment.

"Giving judgment," he read, *"the learned deputy observed that the plaintiff had alleged that Mrs. Gallop was a very difficult customer to fit. Having seen Mrs. Gallop in the witness-box he could well believe it."*

"Well?" said Eleanor accusingly.

"What's wrong with that? It was perfectly true. Mrs. Gallop was the most cantankerous female I've seen for a long time. She found fault with everything. I don't think the dressmaker has yet been born who could have made anything that she would admit was a proper fit. My remarks were perfectly just, and very mild in the circumstances." He read the passage through again. "Good Lord!" he murmured. "Does the woman think I was referring to her *shape*?"

"Obviously. Wouldn't anyone?"

"Ridiculous! She must have known I only meant...Now I come to think of it, she was built on rather baroque lines.... Well, it's all most unfortunate, but how was I to know that she was Lady Furlong's household treasure?"

"She wasn't. Mrs. Gallop is Lady Furlong's cook's mother-in-law. When she read what you had said about her in the paper she took to her bed with a fit of hysterics and the cook has gone home to look after her. Now do you see what you have done?"

"I give it up," said Pettigrew wearily. "The sooner Jefferson recovers, the better. Doing justice in such a temperamental neighbourhood is altogether beyond my powers. Now I suppose I must sit down and read this rag from cover to cover to see what other dreadful solecisms I have committed."

Pettigrew was as good as his word. He carefully scanned every column of the *Advertiser*, and was relieved to find no further references to his activities on the bench. One item of local news, however, caused him some little amusement.

"Just listen to this, Eleanor," he said. "*The popular Henry Spicer Museum at the foot of Yew Hill has been enriched by an autographed cartoon of the famous author by the celebrated artist Fly. This has been generously donated by Mr. Humphrey Rose, at present staying in the neighbourhood for the Easter holiday, and to whom the novelist presented it at an early stage in his career. Mr. Rose is well known as an admirer of the works of the bard of Yew Hill.* What a wonderful country is England! Do you suppose that anywhere else on earth a quite celebrated swindler just out of jail would be called well known as an admirer of somebody's books?"

"You forget," his wife reminded him. "That paragraph was probably written by somebody who was at school when Rose went to prison. He has probably never heard of him."

"He has never heard of the cartoonist 'Spy,' evidently. But that's a minor point. What I feel is a bit hot is that a dangerous ruffian should plant himself among us and then pose as a local benefactor."

"Aren't you being rather unfair, Frank? I don't expect he's a bit dangerous after all those years in prison. He probably just wants to live quietly and respectably. I dare say giving things to the local museum is his way of getting back into decent society."

"If the only decent society he gets into consists of readers of

Henry Spicer, it will be a very restricted one. Anyhow, from what I know of him, Rose will never cease to be dangerous. But we shall see."

There was a ring at the front door. Pettigrew went to answer it.

"That will be Mr. Wendon, I hope," Eleanor called after him. "If he has brought the chicken, will you tell him——"

But it was not Mr. Wendon. It was Mrs. Pink. Pettigrew greeted her in some confusion. It was most awkward, he felt, the way that litigants had of bobbing up in one's path as if they were ordinary human beings.

"You want to see my wife, I expect," he said. "Do come in."

"Thank you," said Mrs. Pink, "but I only wanted to leave her the parish magazine. And this note—it's about the bazaar. We have had to change the date, because of the mission week, you know."

"Quite," said Pettigrew, trying to look as if he did know all about the mission week. He noticed that she looked rather tired, and added, "Have you walked all the way here, Mrs. Pink?"

"Yes. But it doesn't matter. I'm used to walking. And this is the last house in East Yewbury. I've only The Alps to visit now, and then all the notices will be out."

Pettigrew was familiar with the village custom by which parish notices were always delivered by hand, whether to save money or through some atavistic suspicion of the reliability of the post, but he was shocked at the idea of this obviously exhausted woman trudging such a distance up such a hill.

"But you'll kill yourself!" he exclaimed.

"Oh no, Mr. Pettigrew, I'm not so easily killed as that. But it is a long way, that I will admit, and if the Vicar wasn't in such a hurry to get the notices out before Easter I'd leave it till I got my bike mended. I had an accident with it, you see, and the people in Didford won't so much as look at it till the holidays are over."

"But surely Todman's garage could——No, I suppose they couldn't, in all the circumstances. Well, Mrs. Pink——"

He was interrupted by the stuttering roar that announced the arrival of Mr. Wendon's jeep. By the time that he had dealt with the important business of the fowl Mrs. Pink had walked away on her long, self-imposed journey.

"You were all wrong about that pig meal, you know," Mr. Wendon observed, as he was counting out the change.

"I'm sure I was," said Pettigrew easily. Oddly, he felt no difficulty in meeting Wendon, whom he had ordered to pay two pounds a month, whereas talking to Mrs. Pink, who owed him the very roof over her head, caused him acute embarrassment.

"By the way, I've paid the money—all of it."

"Good show."

"Not a good show at all—a damned swindle, if you want my opinion. And the chap I got the cash from was a damned swindler too. So long."

He was about to leave when Pettigrew stopped him.

"By the way," he said, "Mrs. Pink was here just now. I suppose you know her?"

"The widow Pink? Of course I do. Who doesn't?"

"Well, she's proposing to walk all the way up to The Alps to deliver some tom-fool message from the Vicar. Are you driving in that direction by any chance?"

"As a matter of fact," said Wendon slowly, "it would rather suit me to go that way. I'll give her a lift up the hill, is that the idea?"

"Splendid! It will really take a load off my mind. You're sure it won't be too much trouble?"

"No trouble at all. I'll pick her up in the lane."

Pettigrew went back into the house warm with the consciousness of having done a kindness. When he told Eleanor of the arrangement he was a little dashed to find it treated in a very matter-of-fact fashion.

"My dear Frank, Mr. Wendon must have seen Mrs. Pink here. He was probably waiting for the chance to take her out."

"Why do you think that?"

"Has it never occurred to you that he had designs on her?"

"Good gracious, no! They're not at all the same sort of people, I should have said."

"Obviously they are not. She is much too good for him. Anyone can see that. But he badly needs somebody to look after him, and she is an excellent housekeeper and must have a little money of her own———"

"Very little," said Pettigrew. "I happen to know exactly how much."

"Even a little would mean a lot to Mr. Wendon. And if he's not interested in her, can you tell me why he should have driven her home from Didford the other day and stayed to tea?"

"Really, Eleanor, after eight years of marriage I had begun to think I knew something about you, but you continue to surprise me. Since when did you develop into a village gossip?"

"I am nothing of the sort, Frank. I simply listen to what I am told. Lady Furlong has been full of the affair for the last fortnight."

"And where does Lady Furlong get all these precious details from?"

"That is the tragedy. She used to get them from her cook. Now, thanks to you, there will be no more of them."

"This is terrible. The least we can do is to supply the deficiency ourselves to the best of our feeble powers." He took up the field-glasses. "There is just one stretch of the hill road which you can see from here, where it crosses the shoulder. They should be nearly there by now.... Yes, there they go," he exclaimed a moment later. "Enveloped in a cloud of blue smoke. No, I am sorry to report her arm is not round his waist. She is holding on for dear life while he buckets over that rough patch by the corner.... They've gone behind the trees now." He put the glasses down. "And some people call country life dull!" he exclaimed.

"My mother's out, I'm afraid," said Godfrey politely to Mrs. Pink. "But I'm expecting her back any time. Won't you come in?"

"I won't trouble her, thank you very much," said Mrs. Pink, with the air of one repeating a well-learned lesson. "It's only a notice from the Vicar about the bazaar. We find we've had to change the date."

"I'll tell her, then. I'm afraid it will only be of academic interest to her, though. I mentioned that matter of her taking a stall, and she turned it down flat, as I thought she would."

"I quite understand," said Mrs. Pink.

Mr. Wendon meanwhile was rummaging in the back of the jeep.

"I expect your mother could do with a dozen eggs over Easter," he remarked, producing a battered cardboard box.

"Thanks; I expect she could. Wait a bit, though—aren't they supposed to be on the ration, or something?"

"'Supposed' is the word. Just give them to your mother with my compliments and she won't ask any questions."

"Look here, sir," said Godfrey, going rather pink, "I dare say you'll think I'm a fearful prig, but I'd much rather not take them. You see, I had a bit of an argument with Mother about—well, about a rather similar thing only a day or two ago, and I should look rather an ass if she came home and found I'd been taking in eggs off the ration. So do you mind frightfully if I say, No?"

It was clear from Mr. Wendon's expression that he did mind. He returned the box to its place in silence and climbed back into the driving-seat. He fiddled with the starter for a moment, and then said abruptly: "Is that blighter Rose anywhere about?"

"No," Godfrey told him. "Mr. Rose went to London yesterday. I don't know when he'll be back."

"Very well, young fellow-my-lad. I'll just wait here till your mother comes back. Then we'll see who looks an ass." He turned to Mrs. Pink. "What about you, Mrs. Pink? Do you mind waiting?"

"Oh, I shan't wait, thank you, Mr. Wendon. I shall walk home through the Glade. It's downhill all the way."

Grethe appeared at Godfrey's elbow.

"Mr. Godfree, I have put the tea for you in the drawing-room. Mrs. Ransome said not to wait for her."

62

"Oh, thanks awfully, Grethe. I'll come along now." Godfrey was about to go into the house when a thought struck him. "Mrs. Pink," he said, "why don't you come in and have tea before you go? It's awfully dull having meals alone—I mean—that's a rotten way to put it, but I'd love you to come."

"It's very kind of you, Mr. Godfrey," said Mrs. Pink doubtfully, "but I don't know if I should, really——"

"It's quite all right. Grethe always makes much more than I can eat, anyway. Grethe! *Noch eine Tasse, bitte!*"

Mrs. Pink found herself being swept inside The Alps before she well knew what was happening.

"I shan't come in, thank you," said Mr. Wendon to Godfrey's retreating back. He shrugged his shoulders as the door closed behind them. As always, he gloomily resigned himself to unfair dealing. There were, he knew, half a hundred things at his holding that required his urgent attention, but he had said that he would wait for Mrs. Ransome, and wait he would—for a few minutes, at any rate. From behind his seat he produced a flask of whisky and poured himself out a dram. The requirements at the holding began to seem less urgent. Then he took from his pocket a creased copy of the *Didford Advertiser*. His lack-lustre eyes brightened as he observed that the front page carried advertisements of no fewer than three farm sales. He began to read with absorbed concentration.

Mrs. Ransome had been to a lunch-party at Markhampton. After lunch she had been induced to play canasta, which had not been good for either her pocket or her temper. It was with somewhat ruffled spirits that she returned home, to be greeted by strange sounds proceeding from her seldom-used piano. Godfrey, who had been endeavouring to enlist Mrs. Pink's support in a campaign to induce the Vicar to revert to the Cathedral Psalter in place of its new-fangled rival, the Oxford Psalter, was at that moment driving home his point by a practical illustration which left Mrs. Pink as mystified as it would probably have done King

David. The music—to give it a charitable name—stopped abruptly as she entered the room.

"Well, Godfrey!" she exclaimed. "I see you've been having a party. And Mrs. Pink! How very, *very* kind of you to call. I am so sorry that I wasn't in to receive you."

From the saccharine sweetness of his mother's manner Godfrey gathered at once that he had blundered badly in inviting Mrs. Pink into the house. In some confusion, he embarked on a rambling explanation of what had happened.

"Oh, please don't explain!" Mrs. Ransome protested. "I always think explanations are so tiresome, don't you, Mrs. Pink? All that I do gather is that kind Mr. Wendon has brought me a dozen eggs, and that at least is satisfactory. There was rather an upset the last time he came here, and I was afraid he had deserted us. Do you find yourself terribly short of eggs, Mrs. Pink? Or perhaps you keep your own hens?"

"But he didn't bring the eggs, Mother—that's just the point. At least, he did bring them, but I didn't like to take them. He's waiting outside now to see if you want them."

"You didn't take the eggs? My poor Godfrey, you must be mad. And you left poor Mr. Wendon sitting outside——" And brought Mrs. Pink in, was the only too clearly understood corollary. "But where is he now? He certainly was not outside when I put the car away a moment ago." She turned to Grethe, who came in at that moment with a fresh pot of tea. "Grethe, have you seen Mr. Wendon?"

"Oh yes, Mr. Vendon, he is gone now in a hurry. He said he could no longer wait."

"Gone, with all those eggs!"

"Oh no, I took the eggs from him. They are in the kitchen just now."

"Thank heaven for that, at least!" Mrs. Ransome poured herself out a cup of tea. "I couldn't have borne to think that he had gone off with them. To lose a chance of getting anything nowadays is simply criminal. Don't you agree, Mrs. Pink?"

"I don't know, I'm sure, Mrs. Ransome," said Mrs. Pink in her soft, slow voice. "It's hard to say nowadays what's criminal and what isn't, I sometimes think."

It seemed to Godfrey, watching them, that Mrs. Pink had a very curious effect on his mother. It was almost as if she had in some way got upon her nerves. Normally so calm and self-possessed, Mrs. Ransome seemed flustered and uneasy in her presence. Her voice had a harder edge to it than usual, and she caught at the remark as though it contained a personal accusation.

"What a very strange thing to say!" she exclaimed. "I should have thought it obvious that when I said 'criminal' I only meant——Oh, must you go?" she added, for Mrs. Pink had risen and was looking at the clock that hung over the mantelpiece.

"I ought to be on my way," said Mrs. Pink, still looking at the clock. "I wanted to call in at the Vicarage by six. That clock loses a little, doesn't it?"

"My little French clock?" It seemed that Mrs. Ransome could not stop talking. "Yes, it does—about a minute and a half a day, I suppose. It's a pretty thing, isn't it? I've had it for years. My husband gave it to me."

Mrs. Pink turned round and looked her full in the face.

"Oh no, Mrs. Ransome," she said. "Not your husband."

Mrs. Ransome's face had gone a bright scarlet.

"I think you are trying to be impertinent," she said in a strangled voice.

"I'm sorry, Mrs. Ransome; I'm sure I didn't mean to be any such thing. Goodbye, Mr. Godfrey, and thank you for the tea."

With unimpaired dignity Mrs. Pink walked deliberately out of the room.

"Godfrey, show that woman out!" Mrs. Ransome commanded.

Godfrey reached the front door just behind Mrs. Pink. He was about to open it for her when the doorbell rang. Mr. Todman's car was outside and Mr. Todman himself stood on the step, a suitcase in his hand.

"Mr. Rose asked me to leave this," he said. "He's on his way up from the bottom of the hill. Said he wanted a walk."

Godfrey took the suitcase from him, but before he could say anything Mr. Todman had turned round to call after Mrs. Pink, who had slipped past him while he was speaking.

"Mrs. Pink!" he called. "I want a word with you! Mrs. Pink, I say!"

Moving more quickly than was her wont, Mrs. Pink had already got halfway to the gate. She paid no attention to his call.

"Mrs. Pink!" roared Mr. Todman again. He climbed back into his car and drove furiously up the short drive. But by the time he reached the gate Mrs. Pink had already gained the road and turned sharp off it on to the footpath that led steeply downhill towards the Druids' Glade. Watching, Godfrey could see the top of her shapeless blue straw hat bobbing down the path. He could also hear Mr. Todman shouting after her, but he could not distinguish the words.

Carrying the suitcase, Godfrey returned into the house. He found his mother standing by the drawing-room fireplace.

"If ever you let that woman into my house again——" she began, then broke off abruptly. "What have you got there, Godfrey?"

"It's Mr. Rose's suitcase. He's walking up the hill, Mr. Todman says."

"I shall go down and meet him then. I must have some fresh air!"

"Shall I come with you, Mother?"

"Certainly not!"

Feeling thoroughly miserable, Godfrey went upstairs, left the suitcase in the spare room, and then went to his own. Everything seemed to be going wrong, and in some way it appeared to be all his fault. That his mother should decide to take a walk of her own accord seemed the strangest thing of all. She must be very badly upset indeed.

*   *   *

Pettigrew's field-glasses were ranging the hill again.

"Hullo!" he said. "Here comes Mrs. Pink. She's walking home by herself. That doesn't bode well for the progress of Mr. Wendon's romance."

"Frank," said Eleanor, "I wish you'd stop wasting your time at the window. I want you to come and attend to the tap in the kitchen. I think it needs a new washer."

"Just a moment. She's taking the steep way down through the Glade, I believe. Yes, I thought so. How that blue hat of hers shows up! Now she's just reached the line of the yews. 'Beneath those rugged elms, that yew tree's shade, Where heaves the ground——' There! We've seen the last of her. You were saying, my love?"

8

Litter in the Glade

A little before ten o'clock on the morning of Good Friday two men were making their way up the Druids' Glade by the steep path that runs from behind the hotel to the top of the hill. They had the place to themselves, although the easier slope up the bare north face of the hill was already dotted with the advance guard of the army of holiday visitors. The Glade, popular though it is, does not really come into its own until the afternoon, when the returning multitudes scramble and slip down the steep path as the most direct route to the railway station and the bus-stops in the valley. But the way is not entirely precipitous. On and near to the path are fairly level stretches, affording admirable sites for picnics. Their popularity was attested even now by mounds of strewn paper, ice-cream cartons and empty bottles.

The presence of the two men in the Glade that morning was directly related to the offerings with which the visitors had chosen to express their love of nature. Their mission was the important one of selecting a site and erecting thereon a litter basket. Colonel Sampson, who led the way, had been chosen for the task by his fellow committee members of the Friends of Yew Hill because, as a soldier, it was thought that he would have the requisite "eye for country". Mr. Tomlin, who followed him, his back bent double beneath the load of the litter basket, came because he had no choice in the matter. He was the Keeper of the Hill and paid for the job. To judge from what could be seen of his face, he did not think much of this aspect of it.

Unencumbered by anything but a sense of responsibility, the Colonel strode briskly ahead, pausing now and then impatiently for Tomlin to catch up with him. He was a lean, wiry man with fierce-looking, bushy brows, beneath which he gazed out on the world through a pair of mild, innocent brown eyes. Presently he stopped, moved a few paces from the path and drove his stick into the ground beside a pile of débris.

"This is the place, I think," he called down to Tomlin.

Tomlin staggered slowly up the hill to where he stood, laid down his burden and wiped the sweat from his forehead with his sleeve.

"If you say so, Colonel," he said.

"It's the strategic point," the Colonel explained. "There," he pointed to the other side of the path, "is the Arch-druid's Tree, or whatever silly name they choose to give it. Mentioned in all the guide-books and always a focus for trippers. Here," he gesticulated southwards, "is the best view on this side of the hill. You can distinctly see Markhampton cathedral spire in clear weather. I dare say you've noticed it yourself. Climbers up or down the hill stop here for a breather. You can tell that by the mess they leave behind. Then you will see that three paths converge just above where we are standing: one skirting the side of the hill down to the Didford road, one leading up to the top of the hill near The Alps, and the other—where does this path take you, Tomlin?"

"To the car-park, sir, near the last bend of the hillroad."

"Quite so. Well, whichever way they come, they won't be able to avoid the basket if we put it here. No, man, not there," he added as Tomlin upended the basket on the green patch where they stood. "That ruins the view. Put it behind that bush.... Steady on, though, that won't do either. It won't be sufficiently visible to people coming down the hill. They'll lose heart and chuck their stuff away before they get to it. If we were to put it *there*, now...No, that looks dreadful. This is a bit more difficult than I thought. What do you think, Tomlin?"

Tomlin showed no desire to express an opinion.

"I don't know, I'm sure," he said doubtfully.

"Come, come, you must have some views on the matter. It's an important question."

"Well, if you really want to know what I think, Colonel, I don't think it makes a ha'p'orth of difference where you put it."

"What d'you mean?"

"They won't use it, sir, wherever it is. If you was to walk round the hill holding the basket under their noses like a collection bag in church, they still wouldn't take no notice. They'll go on throwing their filth on the ground because that's the way they've been brought up, and no amount of baskets won't teach them any different."

"I'm afraid you're a cynic, Tomlin," said the Colonel. Having uttered what he felt to be the ultimate reproof, he dismissed the objection from his mind. "I think here would do, just on the edge of the slope."

Tomlin shook his head.

"No, sir," he said firmly. "That would just be putting temptation in their way. Two years ago Lady Furlong would have me put one in a place like that, and the very first week-end they just took and rolled it down the hill. I don't see myself going down to the bottom of that and fetching it up every week-end. If you're going to put it anywhere, I should have it where those cigarette cartons are now. It's handy to the path and won't be too much trouble to bring down when it wants emptying."

The Colonel instantly found fault with Tomlin's suggestion and made a counter-proposal. After ten minutes or so of more or less good-tempered argument he finally chose a site, which happened to be the one which Tomlin had selected. The basket was finally set up in its place, and he stood back to contemplate it.

"It looks a bit empty," he remarked. "Hadn't we better put something in—a sort of nest-egg, you know?"

Diving beneath a bush, he brought out an armful of newspapers and a quantity of orange peel, which he ceremonially dumped into the receptacle. He was about to go for more, when Tomlin stopped him.

"That'll be enough to give her a start," he said. "If you start trying to pick up all the muck there is lying about, she'll be full before anyone else can use it—if anyone ever does, which I doubt."

The Colonel looked round him in despair.

"It's hopeless," he said. "There's stuff on the ground wherever you look."

"Well, sir," said Tomlin philosophically, "that's what they are like. All I can say is, things aren't so difficult as they are on the other side of the hill. There, the stuff lies about just anywhere. They do keep to the paths more here. It makes things easier when you come to scavenging."

"Maybe," said Sampson. "All the same, I think you'd find some queer things if you were to look under some of these trees." Stooping down, he peered beneath the lower branches of the Arch-druid's Yew. "There you are!" he exclaimed. "Under that fallen tree. A great heap of rags, or something."

Tomlin also stooped down and looked in the same direction. He looked long and carefully before he spoke. "I don't think it's rags, Colonel," he said, and walked slowly towards the object they had seen. The Colonel followed him, a sudden chill foreboding at his heart.

Some twenty or thirty yards higher up the hill, a yew, smaller in size than the Arch-druid's, but of considerable girth, had stood until blown over by a gale some years previously. Not entirely uprooted, with the tenacity of its kind it had continued to live after a fashion, and a dense screen of green shoots had

71

sprouted from the recumbent trunk. The lie of the land had left a natural hollow beneath one of the main branches. Mrs. Pink's head and shoulders filled neatly into the depression. It was her feet, stuck stiffly out beyond the surrounding leaves, that had told Tomlin that what they had glimpsed at a distance was something more sinister than a heap of rags.

The two men stood looking down at the body in silence for what seemed a very long time. At last Tomlin spoke.

"She didn't get there by herself, Colonel," he said. "Somebody must have put her there."

The Colonel nodded. "Poor woman!" he said. "Mrs. Pink, of all inoffensive people! It must have been some homicidal maniac.... Well, Tomlin," he went on, "I've seen a good many corpses in my time, and I don't need a doctor to tell me that there's nothing we can do for her. You're an ex-policeman. What's the drill now?"

"Notify the station, sir, and meanwhile disturb nothing," replied Tomlin promptly. He looked back the way they had come. "I'm afraid it's a bit late in the day to talk about disturbing nothing, though," he added.

"What do you mean?"

"Well, sir, if the body was brought here from below—and I reckon it's a sight too steep to carry it down from above—that means we must have walked over the very way the fellow took. What's more, if Mrs. Pink was killed on the path, ten to one it will be just where we've been cavorting round with that litter basket. The ground's hard enough as it is, but any prints they do find there will be yours and mine, I'm thinking."

"Well, standing here won't improve any clues there may be," the Colonel remarked. "We'd better get a bit farther away."

They retraced their steps carefully to the giant yew.

"One of us had better stay here to scare off any trippers that may come along," he said. "Dash it, I believe there's one coming now."

Sure enough, from above could be heard a rattle of dislodged pebbles and a moment later the sound of footsteps. They ceased to be heard as they reached the grassy platform where the litter basket had been erected. A moment later Godfrey Ransome came into view round the stem of the great tree. He was walking slowly now, looking at the ground, and had walked almost into Colonel Sampson before he was aware of him.

"Oh, sorry!" said Godfrey. "I didn't see you."

"Are you looking for something?" asked the Colonel.

"Actually, I am. Without any particular expectation of finding it, though. But one does one's best."

Godfrey moved on towards the farther side of the tree, still questing the ground.

"Not that way, if you please, sir!" said Tomlin.

"Good Lord! Why on earth not? Is anything the matter?"

"Yes, sir, there is. You're young Mr. Ransome from The Alps, aren't you?"

"Yes. Of course, I know you. I've seen you about on the hill, often."

Tomlin looked at the Colonel and nodded. Sampson cleared his throat.

"As you're by way of being a local and not one of these damned trippers, there's no harm in mentioning it," he said. "There's been a—an accident in there. I'm just on my way to tell the police."

"An accident?" Godfrey's face looked troubled. For once he looked younger than his seventeen years. "I say, sir, it isn't anything to do with Mrs. Pink, by any chance?"

"And why should *you* think it should be anything to do with Mrs. Pink?"

"Oh God!" The boy was nearly breaking down. "Then it is! This is just too bloody awful for words! I knew something had happened, but——"

"Pull yourself together," said Sampson in a not unkindly tone. "Mrs. Pink has—met with an accident, shall we say?—and is lying in there now. The police have got to be told. Now, I'm not

73

entitled to ask you anything, but questions will be asked, and one of them will be: how did you know it was her?"

"I didn't know, of course," said Godfrey, more calmly. "It was just a silly guess on my part—I never dreamt it could be true. It was simply that she wasn't at early service this morning, which didn't seem a bit like her—I go pretty regularly, you know, and she's always there. So on my way back I nipped round to her cottage to see if she was all right, and I couldn't get any answer. I suppose I ought to have done something about it, but I thought I'd only make a fool of myself making a fuss about nothing, so I came straight home to breakfast. What has happened, do you suppose, sir?"

"That's for the police to find out. You'd better come with me. Tomlin, you'll stay here."

Taking the boy by the arm, the Colonel plunged down the hill. Godfrey blew his nose violently.

"You know, sir," he said, "she was easily the nicest woman I ever knew."

Sampson suppressed a smile. It was funny to hear a boy of seventeen talk like that. All the same, he reflected, the lad might live to seventy and still find no reason to change his opinion.

9

First Enquiries

Detective-Superintendent Trimble, the humourless, ambitious head of the Markshire plain-clothes force, arrived on the scene about noon. The news of the discovery had reached him at his home, where he was enjoying a few days of leave, and he would have been perfectly justified in leaving the preliminary investigations in the hands of the divisional police at Didford Parva; but this was not Trimble's way. The last sensational case of murder in which he had been concerned—that of Lucy Carless at Markhampton—had earned him, somewhat luckily, his promotion from the post of Inspector of the city division to his present high eminence, and he yearned for fresh worlds to conquer. He was not sorry to find, as soon as he left his car at the foot of the hill, that this enquiry would be conducted in the full glare of publicity.

The Druids' Glade, for some distance on either side of the spot where the body lay, had been sealed off by the police who first arrived in answer to Colonel Sampson's message. Hikers proceeding up or down the hill had naturally stopped to stare and speculate at what was going on. The news that part of the hill was temporarily out of bounds had spread. Naturally, this was quite enough to make the forbidden territory an irresistible attraction. The presence of police in force and the arrival of an ambulance added to the excitement. The residents at the Druids Hotel turned out to see what was going on. Eager young men and women plunged into the undergrowth in an effort to dodge the police cordon. Children swarmed everywhere. Trimble, pushing his way through the throng to gain access to the path, observed without dissatisfaction that several press photographers were on the spot already.

The well-tried routine of police investigation was already under way when he arrived. The body had been photographed *in situ* from every available position and the police-surgeon had made his preliminary examination. His report was perfectly straightforward. Mrs. Pink had been dead upwards of twelve hours, possibly as long as twenty. She had been killed by a violent blow that had shattered the back of her skull, producing almost instantaneous death. The familiar words "a blunt instrument" trembled on his lips, but Trimble cut him short.

"Would there be much blood?" he asked.

"That would be impossible to say for certain until I have made a thorough investigation," the doctor told him. "I should expect the weapon employed to be fairly well covered in blood, naturally. Whether the assailant would himself be marked would depend largely on his distance from her at the time—in other words, on the length of the weapon employed."

"Quite." Trimble turned to the officer who had been in charge pending his arrival. "Well?" he asked.

Detective-Sergeant Broome was a depressed, elderly man with a drooping moustache. Of more than average competence, he might have been a first-class officer had it not been for his wife. Her shortcomings as a cook were responsible for his chronic dyspepsia, while her consistent nagging had deprived him of any faith in his own abilities. Consequently he had failed to gain promotion and was now resigned to serving out his time in a subordinate rank, to doing an immense amount of work and seeing others gain the credit.

"There's blood on the ground here," he said, indicating a patch of grass which he had marked out with improvised pegs. "Just a spot—if it is blood. The lab. will have to verify it, of course. Then if you follow along this way, sir, I think you can pick up a trail to where she lies. The ground's all been trampled; but I fancy you can see the marks of her heels where she was dragged along...." He sighed, belched softly, and added, "I dare say I'm only being fanciful as usual. It won't show up in a photograph, anyway."

Trimble examined Mrs. Pink's shoes.

"You're right about her being dragged along," he said. "Now let's see if we can work out what happened...."

It did not take the Superintendent very long to establish to his own satisfaction what had occurred. Mrs. Pink had been struck down from behind at a point just below where the three paths met opposite the Arch-druid's Yew. From there she had been dragged some twenty yards off the path to the place where she had been found. Her bag—a large, shabby affair of black leather—lay beside the body. It proved to contain, besides a few odds and ends, four copies of the Yewbury parish magazine, three circulars relating to the date of the summer bazaar, and a purse with £2 3s 4 1/2d. Robbery had evidently not been the murderer's motive.

So much was clear. What remained uncertain was the direction in which either assailant or victim had been travelling at the time of their encounter. The path up from the foot of the hill and the three tracks that converged on the plateau marked by the Arch-druid's Tree were alike in being steep and stony. Successions of tourists had worn away the soil to the barren chalk beneath, and it was vain to seek for footprints there. As to the scene of the crime itself, it had, as Broome pointed out, been well trampled. By an evil chance, one of Colonel Sampson's selections for a site for the litter basket had been exactly where the initial blood spots had been found, and he and Tomlin between them had effectually masked any traces that might have existed.

Trimble ordered the body to be removed to the mortuary,

providing thereby an agreeable highlight to the Easter holiday of innumerable campers, hikers and family parties who witnessed the slow descent of the stretcher to the road below. He then directed an intensive search of the area surrounding the presumed scene of the crime. While this went forward he interviewed Colonel Sampson and Tomlin. They had already given statements to Sergeant Broome and were now patiently awaiting any further questions that might be put to them by the Superintendent. Trimble did not keep them long. Broome had already extracted from them all that appeared relevant to the case.

"You recognized this woman, I understand?" he said to Sampson.

"Mrs. Pink? Oh, certainly—a most excellent woman."

"Had she any relations that you know of?"

"I never heard of any. She was a very solitary person. A widow, of course."

"Somebody will have to identify her at the inquest."

"I could do that—so could Tomlin, for that matter—or anybody in the neighbourhood. She was a very well-known figure."

"We usually find that a next-of-kin comes forward," said Trimble. "There aren't many really solitary people in the world. Had she any enemies that you know of?"

"None," said the Colonel firmly.

"That's true," added Tomlin.

"Very well. Now is there any other information you can give me, apart from what is in your statement here, Colonel Sampson?"

"No."

"You, Mr. Tomlin?"

"No, sir."

Trimble looked round him thoughtfully for a moment before dismissing them. His eye lighted on the litter basket, now displaced from the position which the Colonel had selected with such anxious care.

"This was the thing you brought up here this morning, was it not?" he added.

"That is right," said Sampson.

"Didn't you bring it up empty?"

"Of course."

"Then, if there has been nobody here since except your two selves, why has it got litter in it now?"

"That was my doing," the Colonel explained. "I thought a bit of stuff in there might encourage the fellows to use it—sort of nest-egg principle, you know."

"I see. And where did you get the stuff from, sir?"

"Oh, it was just lying around," said Sampson vaguely. "Under this bush, wasn't it, Tomlin?"

"Then we'd better have a look at it, just in case you picked up something important by mistake."

Taking up the basket, the Superintendent held it upside down. The rubbish so conscientiously collected a few hours before poured out on to the ground. Going down on hands and knees, Trimble began to sift it carefully. In the presence of an audience he automatically exaggerated the detail of his normally painstaking methods. Every rotting morsel of orange peel was examined, every scrap of newspaper unfolded and scanned, before being put on one side. The Colonel, whose army career had taught him to recognize eyewash when he saw it, yawned openly. And then—to the astonishment of everybody, of Trimble not least—something actually came of the search. Trimble had reached nearly to the bottom of the pile, which had been the top when it lay in the basket. He picked up a large sheet of paper loosely crumbled into a ball. As he did so something fell from its folds—something small and very bright in the sunshine.

The Superintendent picked the little object up and rose to his feet.

"What do you make of that, sir?" he asked the Colonel.

Sampson saw on the officer's extended palm a diamond-stud ear-ring.

"Mrs. Pink never owned anything like that," he said with assurance. "It must have been dropped by someone walking on the hill."

"Probably. If so, its loss will have been notified. I should reckon that diamond is worth a hundred pounds at least." He unfolded the newspaper ball. "*Evening News*, two days old," he commented. "The ear-ring dropped on to the paper, so it must have been lost since then. Well, even if this has nothing to do with the case we shall have done someone a good turn." He began to put the litter back again into the basket.

"I wonder, Colonel, if it was that that young Ransome was looking for?" remarked Tomlin.

"And who may young Ransome be?" Trimble asked sharply.

"A very nice young fellow," said Sampson defensively. "He happened to come along while Tomlin and I were here, and he went down with me when I telephoned for the police. He knew Mrs. Pink and was very much upset when he heard what had happened."

"Where is he now?"

"I sent him off home. He's only a lad, and I didn't think——"

"Home? Where is that?"

"The Alps, up at the top of the hill."

"The middle one of those three paths above leads there, doesn't it? And he was looking for something, you say? Why didn't you mention that sooner, sir?"

"Because it hardly seemed to have any bearing on the matter," said the Colonel stiffly. "And it still doesn't seem to me to have any bearing, in my humble opinion."

There was something rather impressive about the Colonel, mild though his manner was. Trimble had been prepared to be rude, but, looking into those candid brown eyes, he thought better of it.

"You will be wanting to get away, I expect," he said. "I needn't keep you any longer. Good day, sir."

*　　*　　*

80

An hour later Trimble in his turn prepared to leave. The neighbourhood had been systematically searched without further result, and it seemed clear that nothing was to be gained by staying longer. The interested crowds had thinned away into a few scattered knots of hardy spectators. The residents of the Druids Hotel had vanished in response to the imperious call of the lunch-hour. The hill had begun to revert to its normal Eastertide animation.

Trimble was exchanging a few last words with Broome, before returning to headquarters, when he was aware of a disturbance from the path that skirted the southern face of the hill. A babel of high-pitched voices could be heard, mingled with the deeper tones of the officer whose duty it was to prevent any approach by that way to the scene of operations.

"Now you push off before you get into trouble!" Trimble heard.

"But we've got something!" protested a shrill voice. "'Aven't we, Alf? Go on, show it to 'im!"

"Look, sir, blood on it and all!"

"Now you run along——"

"Just look at it, sir!"

"You ask the Super—'e'll give you promotion if he sees it."

"Don't you want your stripes, guv'nor?"

"Look! Blood, I'm telling yer!"

Trimble walked up to the scene of the disturbance. Four grimy urchins, their ages ranging from about eight to twelve, were leaping up and down in excitement on the path. They set up a cheer at his appearance.

"Mister!" screamed the eldest, brandishing a long stick in his hand. "Mister! Just look what we found! Just look——" Trimble held out his hand without a word and examined the object which was eagerly thrust into it. It was a heavy piece of wood nearly four feet long. He noticed at once that it was not in its natural state but had been shaped for a purpose. He judged it to be the corner post of a fence. One end had been sharpened and had at some time been in the ground. The other...He examined it as best he could, surrounded by the jostling, excited children.

"That's blood, ain't it, mister?"

"Garn, I tell yer it ain't—blood's redder'n that, ain't it, sir?"

"Not when it's dry, it ain't. It goes a sort of chocolate, don't it?"

"D'yer think that's what he killed her with, mister?"

"Yes," said the Superintendent suddenly, "I do."

An ecstatic squeal of delight greeted the announcement.

Trimble turned to Broome.

"Let the lab. have this at once," he said. "No need to waste time fingerprinting it. But handle it carefully. There may still be some bits of hair or bone left on the end, though I doubt it, after what it's been through."

He turned to the largest and most vocal of the boys.

"Where did you find this, sonny?" he asked.

"I didn't find it, mister. Barry did. 'Ere, Barry, you tell 'im. Go on! 'E won't eat yer!"

The smallest of the children was pushed unwillingly forward. He stood dumbly in front of the Superintendent, wiping his freckled nose with the back of his dirty hand.

"Well, Barry, where was it?" said Trimble gently. But Barry, oppressed by the sudden publicity thrust upon him, still said nothing.

Trimble gave it up.

"You'd better show me," he said.

The group came to life again with a series of happy yelps.

"I'll show you, mister!"

"Right down 'ere, it is!"

"Come on, Ernie, I'll race yer!"

Following as fast as he could, the Superintendent saw the boys dash down the path a short way and then vanish into the bushes over the sheer hillside. Pursuing them incautiously, he dropped down a miniature precipice and landed uncomfortably in the branches of an elder that had somehow found a foothold in the almost bare chalk face. Below him he could hear excited chattering. He lowered himself painfully ten feet or so and found the boys gathered on a small ledge. He was too much out of breath to ask any questions, but a chorus of voices made questioning unnecessary. Here, and nowhere else, he was informed in ear-splitting tones, the weapon had been found. He looked upwards. The top of the Arch-druid's Tree was just visible. So far as he could judge, the stake, casually tossed from the spot where the assault had taken place, might well have landed thereabouts. It all fitted in very neatly.

"Thank you very much," he said to the boys. "You've been very helpful. Just give me your names and addresses, will you?"

"Will there be a reward, mister?" asked the eldest, when the names had been duly recorded.

"Well, yes, on the whole, I think there will," said Trimble.

He found a couple of half-crowns in his pocket. There would be no difficulty in finding room for them in his expenses sheet, he reflected.

10

Trimble *v.* Todman

The Superintendent returned to his headquarters at Markhampton that afternoon. He had not been there long when a message reached him to the effect that the Chief Constable would be glad to see him, "if it was not inconvenient". Trimble obeyed the summons with the slight feeling of disquiet that an interview with his superior never failed to induce in him. It was not that he disliked Mr. MacWilliam—on the contrary, he was, and always had been, on the best of terms with him. No chief could have been more tolerant, more appreciative of good work done, more understanding. The trouble was that MacWilliam, from Trimble's point of view, was sometimes a little too understanding. Beneath a serious Scottish exterior there lurked a hint of flippancy. Trimble, who—like everybody else—prided himself on his sense of humour, would have had no objection to that, had it not been for the lurking suspicion that the flippancy was on occasion directed at him. Criticism or rebuke he could have borne easily enough; what really got under his fairly thick skin was that he— the hard-working, successful police-officer—was in the eyes of his chief a faintly amusing spectacle.

And all this without a word said! The Superintendent wished

sometimes that MacWilliam would in some way commit himself, so that he could take offence and have things out, man to
man. But how to take offence with a man who had consistently
supported him, applauded his frequent successes, loyally covered up his rare failures and had ended by promoting him to the
highest position in his command? It was impossible. Often Trimble told himself that he was being unreasonable. He owed nothing but gratitude to the man who had helped him up the ladder
of success. If only—if only he could rid himself of the uneasy
feeling that MacWilliam was all the time aware that he looked a
trifle ridiculous, perched up there on the dizzy upper rungs!

"Well, Superintendent," said MacWilliam, "I gather that you
have undertaken a holiday task."

"I thought it my duty to interrupt my leave, sir," said Trimble
stiffly, "in view of the evident gravity of the matter."

"You were absolutely right, of course—absolutely. I should
not myself have ventured to recall you on account of it, but I am
relieved that you thought proper to come of your own accord. I
won't say that Inspector Hodges will not be a shade disappointed at missing the chance of dealing with it in your absence, but
that is unavoidable."

Trimble, who had the poorest possible opinion of Inspector
Hodges, grunted. Before he had time to say anything, however,
MacWilliam went on. "Now I don't want to keep you, because I
know how busy you will be at this stage in the investigation. It's
really only vulgar curiosity on my part until you have a proper
report ready. Just tell me in the fewest possible words about Mrs.
Pink."

As concisely as he could, under that quizzical eye, the Superintendent related the results of his morning's work. The Chief
Constable listened without interruption.

"Very well," he said, when Trimble had finished. "You'll keep
me in touch as the enquiry goes on, of course. So far, it seems to
be a very sordid little affair. But I have a feeling in my bones that
there may be more in it than appears. For your sake, Mr. Trimble,

I'm rather inclined to hope so. It would be a pity for you to have interrupted your holiday if it does not prove worth while. By the way, you haven't told me anything about Mrs. Pink yet."

"There's nothing I can tell you at the moment, sir. She was a widow and lived alone in a little cottage at Yewbury. The witnesses I've seen so far speak very highly of her. There hasn't been time for any relations to come forward yet."

"A widow and lived alone," MacWilliam repeated thoughtfully. "I met her once. She came to see me for a subscription to some good cause or another. I thought her a rather remarkable woman in some respects.... Have you been to her cottage yet?" he asked abruptly.

"I propose going there this evening, sir. After I've——"

"I hesitate to suggest it, Superintendent, but do you think it is altogether wise to postpone going there—even until this evening? She lived alone, remember."

"You think, sir—"

"I think that at the best you may find the place swarming with gentlemen of the press. At the worst—well, you never can tell who might be interested in Mrs. Pink's cottage, could you? I don't propose that you should go there yourself, this moment. But I should recommend that somebody should hold the fort at Yewbury until you can take charge. It is entirely a matter for your discretion, of course, but——"

"I shall go myself, sir," said Trimble shortly. "Now."

Trimble made short work of the fifteen miles or so that separated Markhampton from Yewbury. He took with him the luckless Sergeant Broome, whom he found in the headquarters canteen, enjoying the comparative luxury of a meal for which Mrs. Broome was not responsible. He came into the village just as the Good Friday three-hours service was ending at the church. A small group of worshippers was standing at the lych-gate in earnest discussion. He enquired the way from one of their number and drove on. Turning down the lane, he was relieved to find that the cottage pointed out to him as Mrs. Pink's was deserted and apparently untouched. A small knot of villagers gossiping in the roadway opposite and some children staring in through the closed windows formed the only indication that there was anything out of the way about that unassuming little building.

It was some satisfaction to find that the Chief for once in a way had been wrong, Trimble thought, as he fumbled in his pocket for the key which he had taken from Mrs. Pink's bag. At the same time it was annoying to reflect that he had wasted time which might have been better spent elsewhere by rushing out here on a wild-goose chase. When he got back he would hint to Mr. MacWilliam, very delicately, that there was such a thing as being too clever. The prospect warmed him, and he was already composing the appropriate phrases in his mind as he stepped through the front door into the little sitting-room.

He had hardly had time to look around him when the room suddenly darkened, as the light from the window facing the street was cut off by something large drawing up immediately outside. Looking out, he saw that the obstruction was a big open lorry, piled high with furniture and bedding. Three persons got out of the front of the vehicle: a small, elderly man with bright yellow hair; a younger man, tall, pasty-faced and characterless; and finally a young woman holding a very small baby in her arms.

"Get those traps off as quick as you can," said the small man sharply.

The young man went to the back of the lorry and began untying the tangle of ropes which held the load in place. The woman stood on the pavement watching him. The baby set up a wail. The man who had spoken fumbled in his pocket, produced a bunch of keys and marched straight up to the front door.

"What the devil——?" murmured Trimble.

"Looks as if we'd got here just in time," remarked the Sergeant tactlessly.

The Superintendent reached the door just as it was pushed open from without. The two men almost collided on the threshold.

"'Ere!" said the newcomer. "What's all this?"

"Who are you?" asked Trimble.

"That's a nice question to ask me. 'Oo are you, I should like to know?"

"I am a police-officer."

"Police, is it? Then I'd like to know what you're doing in my house. Have you got a search-warrant?"

"Your house?" Trimble was taken aback. Could he have made some appalling blunder? "This is Mrs. Pink's house, I was told."

"Was—until this morning. I'm the landlord—Todman's the name. She'd 'ad notice to quit months ago. Now she's gone my Marlene's moving in—as she would 'ave done weeks ago if I'd 'ad justice. Just stack those things on the pavement, Charlie," he added over his shoulder to his son-in-law. "We'll have Mother Pink's junk out in a jiffy as soon as the lorry's cleared. You see how it is, mister,"—he turned to the Superintendent with a confident air—"I'm moving in, and that's all there is to it."

"You can't come in here now, Mr. Todman," said Trimble firmly.

"Can't? 'Oo says I can't?" Mr. Todman's voice rose a semitone. "Into my own 'ouse? I've got the law on my side, let me tell you."

The situation was beginning to get alarming. Over Mr. Todman's shoulder the Superintendent could see an interested crowd forming with magical rapidity. Marlene, a picture of misery, with a screaming child at her breast, was the centre of a knot of sympathizers. Her husband, from behind a barricade of furniture on the pavement, was talking vigorously to two men who had all the appearance of press reporters. Somewhere in the background he heard the unmistakable click of the shutter of a camera. Desperately, he sought to temporize.

"Now, Mr. Todman," he said, in the most reasonable tone at his command, "I've got to have a look through Mrs. Pink's things after what has happened. You must understand that. I don't want to have to arrest you for obstructing me in my duty——"

Indeed, he did not. From what he had heard, it seemed that

Todman had an unassailable right to the house. He was anything but sure in his mind as to what was the extent of his power to keep him out. The memory of a recent case in which a police-officer on private property had been successfully sued for trespass crept uneasily into his mind even as he spoke. But Mr. Todman gave him no time for reflection.

"Arrest me!" he squeaked in a piercing falsetto. "Arrest *me!* Are you saying I did the old woman in?"

"Go on, Jesse lad!" called a wit from the back of the crowd. "You give it 'im hot and strong!"

There was a roar of laughter. Evidently the village had settled down to enjoy itself at the expense of the police. It was the most humiliating situation that Trimble had ever found himself in.

"Well?" said Mr. Todman, encouraged by the support from behind. "I'm waiting. Are you going to arrest me or are you not?"

At this moment, to Trimble's immense and ashamed relief, there was a stir in the further ranks of the spectators, and he saw a policeman's helmet making its way through the throng, which scattered submissively at its approach. Beneath the helmet, he knew, was the head of Police-Constable Merrett, one of the oldest, slowest, and, in the Superintendent's estimation, stupidest men in the force. He was a man who typified everything that he deplored in an officer—rusticity, ignorance, lack of ambition or imagination. Trimble had never been so glad to see anyone in his life.

Pushing his bicycle, Merrett slowly approached the front door of the cottage. He had just come off an arduous if unspectacular turn of duty at the scene of the murder at Yew Hill. He was obviously hot, but not apparently particularly bothered. If he was surprised to find his superior officer at bay on Mrs. Pink's doorstep, he did not show it—but his face was in any case always completely expressionless. He leaned his bicycle against the wall of the house, walked up to the door, saluted and said, "Good afternoon, sir!" in the most matter-of-fact way in the world.

Mr. Todman turned round at the sound of a familiar voice.

"Good afternoon, Mr. Merrett," he said in a calmer voice than the Superintendent had heard up till now.

"Afternoon, Mr. Todman."

"This man"—he indicated Trimble with a contemptuous gesture of the thumb—"is trying to tell me I can't come into my own house."

"Ar!" said Police-Constable Merrett reflectively. He sucked his teeth noisily. For a moment there was silence as he indulged in the unusual process of thought. The crowd, Trimble noticed, was now perfectly quiet and orderly. Already it was beginning to thin out, as one after another of its members realized that with the arrival of their trusted policeman—a real policeman in a blue uniform and helmet—the prospects of an interesting riot had faded.

"Ar!" said Merrett again. "Well, Mr. Todman, how d'you think it would be if you was to come inside and talk it over quietly-like with the Superintendent? I'm sure you don't want all Yew-bury to know about your affairs, do you?"

"That's all I want to do—talk it over quietly," snapped Mr. Todman. "Haven't I been saying so all along? But this dam' fool wants to arrest me, or something."

"Now, Mr. Todman, that's not the way to talk to the Superintendent," said Merrett equably. "Get along inside now, and I daresay he won't mind your Marlene bringing the baby in too—it's getting a bit fresh out there in the street. And as for you, Bob Hawkins," he suddenly shouted back, into the crowd, "you've been hanging about here long enough. You buzz off home! And take your friends with you!"

Merrett did not wait to see the result of his last words, but Trimble had not the smallest doubt, as he re-entered the house with a suddenly reasonable Mr. Todman behind him, that Bob Hawkins and his friends had buzzed off home precisely as they had been told.

Once inside the house, with Mr. Todman seated in Mrs. Pink's armchair and his step-grandchild receiving some much-needed nourishment in the back kitchen, Trimble felt himself master of the situation once more.

"You must understand, Mr. Todman," he said, "I have been charged with the investigation of a very serious case—a case of murder. If I'm to do my duty properly I must be able to examine anything the murdered woman possessed. I'm sure you don't want to stand in the way."

Mr. Todman was courteous but determined. In an aggravating fashion, he insisted on addressing his remarks to the constable.

"My old woman," he announced, "won't have Marlene in the house another night, Mr. Merrett. You know how it is up at my place as well as I do. Living like pigs, we are, with the baby screaming its head off, and she with her head bad as it is. The minute she heard about the Pink woman she sent me to get out the lorry and move them out. If I was to go back again this evening with them—well!"

"Ar!" said Police-Constable Merrett.

Trimble became aware of a faint belch behind him. He had temporarily forgotten Sergeant Broome.

"I took the opportunity to go over the house while you were talking at the door, sir," he said. "Nothing of any importance that I can see upstairs, but there's a pile of papers in that desk. I don't suppose they'll help, but it's a surprising pile of papers—that I will say. There's not more than a lorry-load of furniture altogether," he added. "For all the place looks so crowded, it's a very small house."

His words gave Trimble an idea.

"Mr. Todman," he said.

Todman was in the middle of a long-winded confidential chat with Merrett. He looked round sharply at the interruption. Trimble could not but be impressed with the contrast between the malevolence with which he still regarded him and his obvious confidence in the beefy, stupid constable. He changed his mind abruptly.

"Carry on," he said. "I don't want to interrupt you."

He waited patiently while Todman finished the saga of his family misfortunes. Then he said, "Merrett, I want a word with you."

Taking Merrett outside, where the disregarded son-in-law, Mr. Banks, was still keeping vigil over his furniture, Trimble spoke to him earnestly. It took a little time to drive into his head exactly what was required of him, but once he knew his part he played it faultlessly.

"Mr. Todman," said Merrett, returning to the room, "what was you planning to do with Mrs. Pink's home?"

Todman looked disdainfully round him at the "home" of his late tenant, the furnishings whose quality had struck Horace Wendon so favourably.

"Hadn't given it a thought," he said casually. "It's got no business here now, to my way of thinking."

"You might get into trouble if you just left it in the street," Merrett pointed out. "No knowing whose it is now, you know."

He paused to let this sink in before he added, "There'd be room on your lorry to take it away, I suppose."

"Take it where to, Mr. Merrett? I'm not going to have it cluttering up my place, I tell you straight."

"Why don't you ask the Super if you can run it up to headquarters for him? You'd get your regular haulage rates, I expect, and while you're doing it I could be giving Charlie Banks a hand with his stuff. Then Marlene would be all settled in before supper-time and we'd all be happy. What d'you say?"

Late that afternoon the Superintendent drove triumphantly into Markhampton, followed by all Mrs. Pink's movable property piled upon Mr. Todman's asthmatic lorry. Late though it was, the Chief Constable contrived to be in his office when he arrived. He came out into the yard just as the last of the furniture was being off loaded.

"Dear me, Mr. Trimble," he said mildly. "When I suggested

that someone should go and look at Mrs. Pink's cottage I didn't expect to have it brought here."

"It proved necessary, sir," said Trimble, stiffly. "The deceased's landlord was very anxious to get possession."

"Mr. Todman? I rather imagined he might, but he was quicker off the mark than I had expected. I read the account of his County Court case, you know. Mrs. Pink's death seems to have come in very handy for him.... A quick-tempered man, Mr. Todman. Did you find him so, Superintendent?"

"I did, sir, somewhat. But I—I managed him."

"So I perceive, and with remarkable success. It is no more than one would expect of you, Mr. Trimble; but, all the same, I think you are to be congratulated."

"Thank you, sir," said Trimble modestly.

11

Percy, Prufrock and Paine

Before he finally left his office that evening Mr. MacWilliam looked into his Superintendent's room to bid him good night. As he had expected, Trimble was still hard at work. On the floor stood several drawers which had been removed from Mrs. Pink's desk. They were filled with papers, neatly docketed and arranged. A small selection from these was on Trimble's table.

The Superintendent looked up as his chief opened the door.

"I wonder if you could spare me a moment or two before you go, sir," he said.

MacWilliam raised his eyebrows. This was unlike his self-sufficient Trimble. One of the things that he liked about the man was that he did not come running to him for advice except when advice was really needed, or plague him with information about details that he could handle himself. There must be something decidedly unusual in these documents to induce him to ask for an interview.

"Of course," he said. "I am at your service, Mr. Trimble."

He led the way back to his office.

"Mrs. Pink seems to have left an unconscionable quantity of paper behind her," he observed, when he was seated once more behind his desk. "It will take you a long time to get it all sorted out, won't it?"

"No, sir," Trimble replied. "She was a very tidy person, and it is nearly all sorted already. Nine-tenths of it is stuff dealing with her work in the parish, and so forth. It's only the personal papers I'm interested in at the moment, and they are quite manageable. There are just two or three of those I thought you would like to see now."

To his astonishment, the Chief Constable detected a tremor of excitement in the other's voice.

"Are they important?" he asked.

"Important, sir, and surprising."

"I am always ready to be surprised, Mr. Trimble. Please go ahead."

"First, sir, I should like you to read this."

Trimble laid a scrawled letter upon the desk. MacWilliam turned it over and examined the signature first.

"The good Mr. Todman," he remarked. "What has he to say to us?" He turned back to the beginning of the letter. "Dated the day before yesterday, I see. 'Mrs. Pink—This is to tell you that I'm getting near desperate, and desperate men are dangerous. Over my dead body you said to me and over your dead body it nearly was on the road last week.' What does he mean by that, I wonder? 'I've made you a fair offer and you've had fair warning and this is the last you'll get. So be reasonable or take the consequences. Your landlord, Jesse Todman.' Short and sweet, Superintendent. I presume that you will be seeing Mr. Todman and inviting his comments upon it?"

"Yes, sir."

"Well——" The Chief Constable suppressed a yawn. "Thank you for letting me see the letter. It seems to provide a very simple explanation for the whole affair, does it not?"

Privately, MacWilliam felt disappointed in his Superintendent. After the promise of sensational revelations Todman's letter seemed decidedly flat. And if, at this time of day, Trimble

95

could really be surprised that a landlord kept out of possession against his will should be in a murderous mood, then he was a far simpler fellow than a man in his position had any business to be.

"Yes, sir," the Superintendent was saying, "a very simple explanation."

The Chief Constable looked up at him sharply.

"Mr. Trimble," he said, "I have in the past from time to time indulged myself in the amusement of leading you up the garden path. It is a reprehensible habit, no doubt, but none the less perfectly in order under the rules. It is, in fine, a privilege to which, as your superior officer, I am entitled. That you should attempt in return to lead *me* up the garden path is wholly inadmissible. Will you please therefore stop wasting my time and produce the other papers you are withholding from me? I warn you that unless they are genuinely surprising the consequences will be serious."

Without a word Trimble laid upon the desk a letter typed upon good paper, with the heading of a firm of City solicitors. It was in fact the letter which Mrs. Pink had received upon the day of the County Court action.

"Percy, Prufrock and Paine!" murmured MacWilliam. "What on earth should they be writing to Mrs. Pink for? 'Dear Madam, We have received notice from Amalgamated Overseas Produce Ltd. that their first issue of Debentures will be redeemed on the 15th proximo. As you will recollect, your holding of this issue amounts to £5,000.' Whew! 'Together with accrued interest and cash in our hands, this will leave the sum of £5,580 6s. 11d. available for re-investment. We attach hereto a selection of securities suggested by our stockbrokers. Bearing in mind the somewhat high proportion of industrial stocks in your present list, we would recommend ...' Etcetera, etcetera. My dear Superintendent, this is fantastic! Are there any more letters like this?"

"Quite a number, sir. I have only made a small selection for you."

"'Bearing in mind the somewhat high proportion of industrial stocks in your present list'—damn it, the woman must have been quite rich!"

"Evidently, sir." Another letter from Percy, Prufrock and Paine was set before the Chief Constable. He stared at it incredulously. "'We have now agreed your surtax assessment with the Special Commissioners at the figure of——' Impossible! Trimble, do you realize what this figure means? She wasn't simply well off, as you and I understand it—she was positively rolling in money!"

"That was what I had gathered, sir."

"Rolling in it! She could have bought up Todman and all his works a dozen times over and never noticed it. What on earth was she doing, living as she did?"

"Well, sir, one does come across cases of misers every now and again—elderly females especially. You'll remember there was that old woman in Pondfields Lane a year or two back."

"I know—she was a typical case. Starved to death in a filthy hovel, with wads of bank-notes stuffed away in the cupboard. By the way, was there any money in Mrs. Pink's house?"

"Not a penny, sir, unless you count the pound or two found in her handbag. She had thirty pounds to her credit in the Savings Bank. I didn't find any other bank account."

"P. P. and P. looked after that for her, no doubt. Was the body well nourished?"

"From what the doctor says, I gather that it was, sir."

"Was her furniture well cared for?"

"Spick and span, sir. A very house-proud woman, I should say."

"Not like the old woman in Pondfields Lane, then. Not like any miser I've ever heard or read of. Besides, a miser wouldn't spend her time working like a slave on causes and committees and things, as Mrs. Pink did. Who ever heard of a miser doing good, except to his heirs? The thing's a contradiction in terms."

"Well, sir," said Trimble. "If Mrs. Pink wasn't a miser, what was she?"

"What was she? Who was she? Where did her money come

97

from? Who gets it now she's dead? And finally, my dear Mr. Trimble, have the answers to these questions anything whatever to do with the only question which really concerns us—who did her in?"

MacWilliam stood up.

"I am going home now," he said. "You have certainly succeeded in surprising me, Superintendent. I hope, for your sake, that you will not succeed in making an arrest over the week-end, for if you do you will deprive yourself of the pleasure of a trip to London in order to get an answer to the other questions from Messrs. Percy, Prufrock and Paine. I assume that their office will have reopened by Tuesday, though from my experience of solicitors you will be almost certain to find that the gentleman attending to the matter is not in the office just now. Still, if you announce your coming beforehand some hapless junior clerk will no doubt——"

He was interrupted by a ring from the office telephone.

"Please answer it, Mr. Trimble," he said. "And tell whoever it is that I have left."

Trimble picked up the receiver and spoke to the constable on duty who had made the call. MacWilliam meanwhile was putting on his hat and coat.

"Who?" said Trimble into the telephone. "He's here now?...What about?...I see...." The Chief Constable was at the door. "Mr. Pettigrew has called, sir," he said to him. "In connection with the case of Mrs. Pink. Shall I tell him you have gone?"

MacWilliam paused in the open doorway. Several years previously he had made use of Pettigrew's unofficial assistance in an investigation of which Trimble was the officer in charge. The affair had ended happily enough, with apologies and forgiveness and a promotion for Trimble as solatium. It had never since been mentioned between them, but he knew that the affront to the officer's professional pride still rankled. Now here was the irrepressible Pettigrew bobbing up again—uninvited this time—when the enquiry was only a few hours old. It was awkward. If

Pettigrew had anything of importance to tell, the Superintendent was the proper person to take his statement without interference. But if, as he suspected, it was merely the case of an amateur presuming on his solitary stroke of luck to push in with his unwanted theories, then the sooner he sent him about his business the better. And Trimble should see him do it. The ghost of professional disloyalty would be laid once for all.

He turned back from the door. "I think we'd better see him together," he said. "Tell them to show him up."

Pettigrew was sensitive to atmosphere. From the moment he came into the room he realized that his appearance there was regarded with suspicion. Without troubling to determine the cause, he decided to make the interview as short as possible.

"I had no intention of troubling you personally, Chief Constable," he said. "Or the Superintendent, for that matter. I am simply here to make a short statement of fact, which may conceivably be of importance."

He noticed with interest the look of relief that passed over MacWilliam's face at his words, and went on:

"I should perhaps begin by explaining that I have been out most of the day and have only just heard of this affair on the six o'clock news. Living where I do, there is normally very little that occurs on the hill without my noticing it at once."

"And your statement of fact, Mr. Pettigrew?" said the Chief Constable frostily.

"My statement of fact arises directly from what I have just said. It is this: Mrs. Pink was last seen alive yesterday afternoon at ten minutes past five precisely."

"By you?"

"By me. And to avoid any possible misconception I may add that it was at a range of some hundreds of yards, through field-glasses."

"Do you suggest that you could recognize her face at that distance?"

"Her face—no, though they are pretty powerful glasses. But I could swear to her hat anywhere. I had seen it at close quarters less than an hour before."

"Where was she when you saw her?"

"On the path leading down from The Alps, just entering the yew wood."

"And what makes you think that you were the last person to see her alive?"

"I apologise. That was an unwarrantable assumption on my part. I should have said that I saw her at the last moment before she went into the wood from which, I gather, she never emerged. Of course, if you have later information as to her movements, then I have been wasting your time."

"On the contrary," said MacWilliam, in a more friendly tone than he had shown up till then. "Your information is very valuable. Do you agree, Superintendent?"

"I do, sir. I should like to ask Mr. Pettigrew whether he is quite sure she was alone when he saw her?"

"Positive. I noticed it particularly, because she had not been alone when she went up to The Alps."

"In that case, sir, I think I must trouble you for a complete statement in writing covering the whole period from the time when, as you say, you saw her at close quarters up to ten minutes past five yesterday afternoon."

The Chief Constable took his cue. "You can use this room if you wish, Mr. Trimble," he said. "I think it is warmer than yours. Good night, Mr. Pettigrew. Thank you for coming along." And he departed.

Half an hour later Pettigrew, his statement completed, read over, signed and witnessed, left the police headquarters in search of a bus to take him home. His way took him past the municipal car-park. A car slid forward from the park and stopped beside him. A voice from within said, "I am driving you home, if you don't mind."

"My dear Chief Constable," said Pettigrew, getting in, "this is a surprise!"

"It had to be," MacWilliam explained. "If Trimble had seen us together it would have been fatal. You see, when you were announced this evening we both thought you had come along to teach us our business again."

"God forbid!" Pettigrew cried. "And you know perfectly well that I didn't——"

"I know you didn't. And it was very stupid of me to think that you would. But you can hardly blame Trimble for doing so. It was a great relief to find that you were a mere witness of fact."

"And that is all I mean to be. Don't you realize how I loathe this business of detection?"

"Excellent!" said MacWilliam approvingly. "You seem to be in a very proper frame of mind. All the same, I'm going to trouble you with one question on what is not a matter of fact, but of opinion."

"I shan't answer it."

"Just as you please. I shall ask it, all the same. Would you say that Mrs. Pink was an altogether normal person?"

"Yes," said Pettigrew promptly, and a moment later, "No."

"I see." The Chief Constable's voice was quite devoid of irony.

"She was normal in the sense that——Look here, do you know anything about forestry?"

"Nothing at all."

"Nor do I. But I know somebody who does, and a very dull dog he is too. But he was talking to me one day at inordinate length and quite uncontagious enthusiasm about a forest in Germany or somewhere which he said was almost normal. I asked him what a normal forest was, and it seems that such a thing doesn't really exist. It means one that is so planted and arranged that—oh, I won't bore you with the details as he did me, rotation and felling and replanting and so on, but a normal forest is a forester's dream, one without any snags to it. Everything in apple-pie order. Do you follow me?"

"I follow. And Mrs. Pink was a dream? Whose?"

"All I am trying to convey is that she was a thoroughly good woman. I don't know whether you call that normal or not. A policeman wouldn't, I suppose. Being what she was, I dare say her behaviour might have seemed abnormal by other people's not so good standards. That's all."

"That is very interesting," said MacWilliam. "You must have known her very well."

"Good Lord!" said Pettigrew. "I believe I only spoke to her twice in my life. I am an ass."

12

Trimble at the Alps

Godfrey Ransome did not go on the hill on Easter Saturday. On that day, as on every day during Bank Holiday week-ends, the inhabitants of The Alps lived in a virtual state of siege. An endless file of small cars and overburdened motor-cycles choked the lane that ran past their gates, while the slopes beyond the garden fence were swarming with holidaymakers on foot. Needless to say, the vast majority of the visitors were tamely content to enjoy the wide stretch of country to which they were by law entitled. Barely one in a hundred thought of throwing their empty bottles into Mrs. Ransome's garden; only a mere handful would attempt to climb the fence to help themselves to her daffodils and primroses; while not more than one party in a day would normally be expected to light a fire in her orchard to brew themselves a cup of tea. Pioneers were ever the exception. But, as always, it is the active minority that counts. So it came about that under his mother's direction Godfrey was spending the morning in a state of peripatetic vigilance.

It was a tiresome waste of time to an intellectual young man who had looked forward to getting in a few hours solid work on his entry for the *New Statesman* literary competition; but to one who had never before lived in a beauty spot it had the attraction of novelty. He had already garnered a varied collection of offerings for the dustbin from various parts of the perimeter, discouraged several small boys from balancing on the palings on the border of the wild garden, and informed two harassed mothers who marched up the drive demanding to be directed to a "toilet" that they would find all their requirements at the tea-gardens farther up the lane. Then followed a temporary lull, while he endeavoured at last to get into the proper frame of mind for literary composition. It did not last long. In a few moments he heard the front gate open once more, and yet another two intruders hove in sight.

The fact that the newcomers were careful to shut the gate behind them was sufficient in itself to differentiate them from any other strangers who had appeared at The Alps that morning. The leisurely speed of their approach made it fairly certain that their errand had none of the urgency that had driven the ladies whom he had recommended to the tea-gardens. They came up to the house as though about to pay a social call—but Godfrey by now knew his mother well enough to be fairly certain that these were not of the type with whom she would be on calling terms.

Godfrey met them halfway to the door. His mother's instructions after breakfast that morning had been, "For pity's sake, Godfrey, keep them out!"; and until he had good evidence to the contrary he was going to assume that these men, like the others, were "them". Before he could say anything, however, the smaller of the strangers spoke.

"Good morning," he said politely. "We are police-officers. Are you Mr. Ransome?"

"Yes," said Godfrey. "Yes—that is—I mean—yes."

It was not, he felt, the way that a man of the world should have replied to such a simple question. There was really nothing in the least alarming in being asked your name by a policeman.

No sensible chap should make a fuss about it. To his fury, he could feel that he was blushing. Luckily, the man did not seem to notice anything unusual.

"My name is Trimble, by the way," he said. "Detective-Superintendent Trimble. My colleague here and I are enquiring into the matter of Mrs. Pink. We understand that she called here on Thursday afternoon."

"Oh yes. She did."

"Then perhaps you wouldn't mind assisting us by answering a few questions?"

"I am at your service, Superintendent." (That was much better. It was what all the chaps in books said, anyway.)

Godfrey led the way into the house. He took them into the dining-room. His mother, he knew, was in the drawing-room on the other side of the house, and he had no intention of disturbing her unnecessarily. Trimble's colleague produced some sheets of official-looking paper which he laid out on the table, where they looked strange against the urbane, polished mahogany, and Godfrey nervously faced his first experience of a police interrogation.

"What time did Mrs. Pink arrive here on Thursday?"

"About half-past four."

A long pause, while the colleague scribbled industriously with a fountain-pen.

"Was there anyone with her when she came?"

"She came in Mr. Wendon's car."

So it went on. It was a surprisingly simple business. Once he had got over the initial discomfort of finding himself the subject of police enquiry Godfrey found himself, rather shamefacedly, enjoying the experience. A reasonable individual such as he was set small store by such things, but it did none the less give one a certain sense of importance. He spoke fluently, and, he felt, with an apt choice of words that should have impressed the Superintendent.

His self-satisfaction was sadly diminished when, the interrogation completed, his statement was read back to him in bald, official English, the flowers of speech shorn away, the bare facts set down in all their crudity. Put that way, his evidence didn't amount to very much after all. It barely covered a sheet and a half of the constabulary foolscap.

He signed at the foot of the statement. Trimble added his signature as witness, and that was that. Then, just as he was folding up the paper preparatory to putting it away, the Superintendent asked him another question.

"You were down near the Arch-druid's Tree yesterday morning, weren't you?"

"Yes, I was."

"Looking for something?"

"Yes."

"Did you find whatever it was you were looking for, Mr. Ransome?"

The Superintendent's expression could only be described as coy. Godfrey was irresistibly reminded of one of his more tiresome aunts about to produce a "surprise" at Christmas-time. He had been a small boy then, and he disliked being treated as a small boy now.

"No," he said, in his most grown-up manner. "Do you want me to describe it to you? I presume that you have found something."

"I have found *this*, Mr. Ransome." The diamond ear-ring glittered on the Superintendent's broad palm.

"Oh, good!" Godfrey's relief at seeing it again swept away his temporary annoyance. "My mother will be pleased."

"You recognize it as Mrs. Ransome's?"

"Of course."

"And when did she lose it?"

The voice was no longer coy. It was distinctly hard and unpleasant.

Godfrey said nothing for a moment. In the brief pause before he answered he had time to feel very frightened, very foolish and very angry.

"I think you had better ask her that," he said finally.

Trimble gave him a long, hard stare. His face was quite expressionless.

"If you put it that way, Mr. Ransome, perhaps I had," he said.

Mrs. Ransome was sitting in her drawing-room sewing when Godfrey entered with the two detectives. She raised her elegant eyebrows at the sight of them.

"What is it, Godfrey?" she asked. "And who are these extraordinary people? I told you not to let anyone in."

"We are——" Trimble began, but Godfrey was determined to be too quick for him.

"This is a policeman, Mother," he said. "He's found your earring."

"Oh, but how clever of you!" Mrs. Ransome exclaimed, laying her sewing in her lap. "You see how much better policemen are at looking for things than ordinary people, Godfrey! Let me see it. Yes—my ear-ring it is. Where did you find it, Constable?"

"Superintendent, madam. Detective-Superintendent Trimble of the Markshire Constabulary. This is Detective-Sergeant Broome."

"I beg your pardon. Well, I'm extremely grateful to you both, all the same. I was going down to the police-station about it today, but I suppose my son told you it was missing."

"It was found, madam, in the course of another enquiry altogether," said Trimble portentously.

"Well, never mind how. It has been recovered, that's the great thing. Er—I *was* going to offer a little reward. Godfrey, dear, my bag is on that table in the window, I think."

"Please don't trouble yourself, Mr. Ransome," said Trimble. "There is, of course, no question of any reward in this case. What I am interested in, madam, is how you came to lose it."

"What an extraordinary question to ask! How does one lose

an ear-ring? If you were a woman and hadn't ever bothered to have your ears pierced, you wouldn't need to be told. It's the most fatally easy thing in the world."

"I have no doubt it is. But are you able to say when and where you lost it?"

"If I was able to say that, I should have been able to find it for myself. But it wasn't stolen, if that is what is bothering you. It dropped off somewhere on the hill the other evening, that's all I know. Was that where you found it?"

"I found it yesterday morning in a litter bin by the Arch-druid's Yew."

"In a litter bin! What an extraordinary piece of luck! I'm sure you never thought of looking there, Godfrey."

"The bin had only been placed there just before. There can be no question of your having dropped it into the bin."

"Well, really, this is very odd. You mean to tell me that someone picked it up and put it into the bin? What strange things some people do!"

"Be that as it may, madam," said Trimble impatiently, "it would appear that this ear-ring was lost in the vicinity of the Arch-druid's Yew."

Mrs. Ransome shook her head vaguely.

"I'm no good at those touristy names," she said. "I'm only a resident, you know. I don't read the guide-books. What do you call the Arch-thingummy's Yew?"

"I mean the large tree about halfway down the hill from here where three paths meet."

"I think I know the place you mean."

"Were you there on Thursday afternoon?"

"I'm not sure. Why Thursday in particular?"

"Was that not the day you lost the ear-ring?"

"Was it?"

"As your son here was looking for it on Friday morning, I presume that you had discovered the loss the previous evening."

"Oh, very well, I expect it was Thursday."

"You met Mrs. Pink here on Thursday, did you not?"

"Mrs. Pink? What has all this to do with her?" Mrs. Ransome seemed genuinely bewildered.

"The body of Mrs. Pink was found on Friday morning, madam, within a few yards of the tree known as the Archdruid's Yew."

"Oh yes, I know. Terrible," said Mrs. Ransome in the hushed tones which a well-bred person sometimes employs in speaking of the recently dead. Then her face changed as an idea suddenly came to her. "Mrs. Pink!" she repeated. "You mean she might have taken my ear-ring with her when she left the house? Godfrey, we never thought of that!"

It was very plain from Godfrey's expression at that moment, as the Superintendent was quick to observe, that he certainly had never thought of any such thing.

"Of course," Mrs. Ransome went on, "she might have taken it accidentally—caught up in her dress in some way. It's always possible. One wants to be charitable to the poor thing after what has happened. But she certainly did behave very strangely that day, didn't she, Godfrey? Inviting herself to tea with you and then being positively rude to me afterwards. When we were hardly more than strangers, in any case! One feels a woman in that mood might have done *anything*. Was she—er—of a certain age, do you know, Superintendent?" she enquired delicately. "Women do sometimes——"

"I know nothing about that at all," said Trimble abruptly. "And I have no reason to suppose that Mrs. Pink stole your ear-ring."

"Oh, very well!" Mrs. Ransome shrugged her shoulders. "It doesn't seem to me to matter much whether she did or not, so long as I have it back."

"This ear-ring, madam," said the Superintendent impressively, "was found within a few yards from the spot where a murder was committed. We know that the murdered woman was last seen alive on the path leading down from this house. You left the house very shortly after she did. I am asking you now to explain your movements from that time."

"Asking me to explain?…Asking *me* to explain! I really think it is about time to ask you to explain! Are you seriously suggesting that I had anything to do with the death of this unfortunate woman?"

To anyone looking at Mrs. Ransome, sitting in her elegant drawing-room, it certainly seemed a very odd suggestion indeed.

"I have not suggested that."

"Well, you have certainly implied it." Mrs. Ransome picked up her sewing and began jabbing her needle into her work with furious concentration. "And if that was not the suggestion I don't know what the point of your question was. And I absolutely refuse to answer anything further except in the presence of my solicitor. And what he will say when I tell him that I've been practically accused of murder because somebody else chose to pick my ear-ring up and hide it in a litter bin I don't know."

"Very well, madam," said Trimble. "If you take up that attitude there is nothing further that I can do. Before I go, however, I should like a word with Mr. Rose."

"He is not here," said Mrs. Ransome curtly, her head still bent over her sewing.

"I understood that he was staying in the house. When did he leave?"

"Yesterday."

"Then where is he now?"

"I have no idea."

"I see, Mrs. Ransome, that you are quite determined not to help us." The superintendent got up to go.

"After the way you have insulted me I don't see why I should." Mrs. Ransome picked up her scissors and snipped off her thread. "I will thank you for my ear-ring," she added. "There is no reason why you should deprive me of my property as well as trying to take away my reputation. Godfrey, show these people out."

"Well, Godfrey," said Mrs. Ransome a few minutes later, with a cheerful smile, "have they gone?"

"Yes, Mother."

"Did you have a look to see if there were any more of those odious trippers about in the garden?"

"Yes, Mother."

"Well, don't go on repeating 'Yes, Mother' like that, you silly boy. Anybody would think you were afraid I should eat you. Was there anybody?"

"Only a couple of children picking daffodils behind the pot-ting-shed, and I got rid of them. There was a police-car waiting for the detectives outside the front gate, and I expect that kept most people away."

"That's one good result of having the police here, anyhow. It was rather fun in a way, though, wasn't it?"

"Mother, I——"

"Yes, Godfrey?"

"Oh, nothing. Only I—I wish you wouldn't."

"Wouldn't what, exactly?"

"Oh—you know."

"Yes," said Mrs. Ransome, smiling sweetly. "You don't express yourself as clearly as usual, Godfrey, but I know, only too well. But sometimes one has to, and I'm afraid I'm the sort of person who rather enjoys doing it. Now for goodness' sake take that hangdog look off your face and go and get the sherry. There's just time for a glass before lunch, and I have an idea that we both need it."

"I wonder, Godfrey," said Mrs. Ransome as she sipped her sher-ry, "who really killed that silly old Mrs. Pink—and why? It would be interesting to know, wouldn't it?"

13

Fresh Light on Mrs. Pink

The inhabitants of Yewbury, apart from the minority whose occupation allowed them to make money out of the week-end visitors, naturally preferred to get away from the village during the Easter holiday. By way of avoiding the crowded slopes of Yew Hill they piled into their baby cars and motor-cycle combinations, launched on to the traffic-choked roads and with one accord made for the sea, where they spent a few happy hours on the crowded beaches of some popular resort, whose inhabitants (apart from the minority engaged in making money out of the visitors) had fled to some inland beauty-spot, such as Yew Hill. It was therefore without surprise that Trimble, on calling at Mr. Todman's garage, learned from the gloomy hireling left behind to operate the petrol pump that the proprietor and his wife, with a cargo of paying passengers, had left at dawn for Bognor Regis and were not expected home before nightfall.

By this time it was well past noon, and the Superintendent suggested to Sergeant Broome that they should lunch at the Huntsman's Inn. The Sergeant, who had been on duty practically continuously since Friday morning, agreed with an alacrity that was a tribute less to his devotion to his work than to his horror of the meal that he would have had to eat at home. A moment later, however, he relapsed into his usual gloom and remarked that the Huntsman's would be sure to be crowded out with tourists.

Trimble sent him in to enquire, and he appeared a moment later, announcing with the relish of the justified pessimist that there was not a table to be had for half an hour and that the joint was off already.

"Very well," said the Superintendent, "then we will wait for half an hour."

"You can't get near the bar," said Broome moodily. "It's packed right out."

"I did not say anything about the bar," retorted Trimble virtuously.

He was, in fact, not sorry to have a little time at his disposal in which to stroll through the village. Himself a townsman, he always felt a little out of his element when faced with a problem that had for its background a community such as Yewbury. Village life, with its close-knit unity masking a hundred subtle social distinctions, its ramifications of blood and marriage ties, its feuds and enmities that could be as old as the parish church or as recent as last year's horticultural show, always had been and remained to him a mystery. The most that a stranger could do was to keep his eyes and ears open for the chance sight or sound that might give him a glimpse into what went on below the surface.

With the patient and thirsty Sergeant Broome in attendance he strolled past the inn down the lane to Mrs. Pink's cottage. The sound of hammering and the wail of a baby from within showed that Marlene and her husband had put the duties of home-making before the delights of the seaside. Outside the house, leaning on his bicycle and gazing earnestly at nothing in particular, was Police-Constable Merrett.

The Superintendent felt irritated at the sight of that placid, bucolic figure. If only he had a really smart man in the village! There must be an enormous amount of background information

113

going begging for an intelligent officer. Merrett would notice nothing that was not right under his nose—and barely that, he reflected, if he continued to star-gaze in that absentminded fashion.

Merrett finally became aware of his superior's approach, drew himself up and saluted.

"Looks as though it was going to turn out fine over the weekend," he remarked genially.

Trimble was not interested in the weather.

"How long have you been stationed in Yewbury?" he asked abruptly.

Merrett gazed skyward once more in the throes of mental calculations.

"Eleven years come Michaelmas," he finally announced, lowering his eyes to the Superintendent's level.

"Then you ought to know the people pretty well?"

"I wouldn't say that, sir. Eleven years isn't all that long to get to know a place, would you think?"

Trimble's mind went back to all that he had accomplished in the past eleven years, and his impatience merged into pity for an existence so eventless and futile.

"How well did you know Mrs. Pink?"

"Not at all, sir," said Merrett with the jovial air of one imparting good news. "She kept herself to herself, you see. Ever since she came back to Yewbury as a widow. Nobody in the village knew anything about her, really. A real mystery woman, you might say. Very rich she was, of course."

"Eh?" said the startled Trimble. "How did you know that?"

"Just common village gossip, sir. Rich as a lord and lived like a miser. That was what made her so unpopular in the place."

The Superintendent felt that he was getting an altogether new picture of Mrs. Pink.

"Unpopular?" he echoed. "I understood that everybody liked her."

"Lord bless you, sir, no! I expect you've been talking to the gentry—Colonel Sampson, Lady Furlong and all that crowd.

They liked her all right—she was that useful. And the Vicar too, 'cos she was always at church. But the villagers didn't like her. It stands to reason. All that money, and living so small—it isn't natural. And then keeping herself to herself the way she did, for all she was born in the village. Mind you, sir, nobody had a word against her, if you understand what I mean. She was a respectable woman—a good woman, you might call her, I dare say. Never an unkind word to anybody, and that useful in the place they'll have a job to manage without her. But as to liking her—no. She was much too quiet. Kept herself to herself, if you follow me, sir."

"Yes," said the Superintendent. "I think you mentioned that point before."

"Well, that's about the size of it," Merrett concluded, gazing up into the sky once more and sucking his teeth reflectively. "And it didn't make her any the more popular keeping Mr. Todman's Marlene out of her house, and her with all that money and all."

"You haven't told me," Trimble reminded him, "how the gossip got about that she had money."

"Well, sir, in a small place like this it's not difficult for things to get about once they start. This one started over *there*." Merrett nodded towards the village post-office, two doors away from where they stood.

"Yes?"

"Telephone calls to London," said Merrett darkly. "Telegrams, even, once or twice. But mostly it was letters. All typed envelopes, I understand—big ones, some of them, the sort you send papers in. And then she'd post them back in envelopes with the address on them all ready printed. Same address every time, they say—London lawyers. Well, sir, anybody can have a letter from a lawyer now and again, but when it's happening all the time what can it mean but money? That's what the village said, anyway. I dare say they was wrong, but that's what they *said*."

115

Merrett looked ostentatiously at his watch and prepared to climb on to his bicycle.

"And if she hadn't got money," he added as an afterthought, "why did Mr. Wendon want to marry her?"

"Did he, indeed?"

"That's what they said, sir. Mind you, it's only common, ordinary village gossip. I'm not saying it's evidence. But Mr. Wendon could do with a wife—and with money too. Everybody knows that. And there he was, giving her rides in that broken-down car of his, dropping into tea, even, they tell me. And that's a pretty remarkable thing for a woman like her. She kept herself to herself mostly, you see."

With a parting salute the constable rode away.

Lunch at the Huntsman, though jointless, was palatable enough. Sergeant Broome was in an almost cheerful frame of mind by the time that it ended.

"It looks to me, sir," he said as they drove away from the inn, "as though this case was simmering down very prettily. Barring accidents, it seems we can reduce it to one of three people. Not so bad, after less than a couple of days' work."

"Three, Sergeant?" said Trimble. "At the moment I make it four."

"I don't get you, sir. You're not counting the boy, surely. A regular softy like that—I wouldn't have said he had it in him."

"Neither should I. Indeed it's on his evidence that I am relying for my four. There's his mother for one——"

"A hard-boiled woman, that. Though I shouldn't have thought this was what you'd call a female type of crime, would you, sir?"

"I should not—but, all the same, until I have some reasonable explanation of that ear-ring I can't leave her out of it altogether. Then we have Todman—we know what his motive was; and if he's the man we're wasting our time prying into all Mrs. Pink's affairs."

"This sort of work is nine-tenths waste of time anyhow, don't you think, sir?" said Broome resignedly. "Not that I mind—I'm used to it at my time of life. Well, if it is Todman I expect we can break him down when we get the chance to talk to him."

"If it is Todman," said the Superintendent reflectively, "he's a very brave man. I don't expect any easy confession from him."

"Brave, sir? There's nothing very brave about clubbing a poor woman from behind, it seems to me. Real coward's trick, I call it."

"Maybe; but you're forgetting that we have already seen Mr. Todman. Assuming that he's the murderer, he acted the part of a brave man then. Just put yourself in his place. You have killed your tenant because in the present state of the law it's the only way you can hope to get possession of your house. You have come round to the place in triumph to gather the fruits of your crime. And the first thing you see when you open the door is a plain-clothes policeman. Don't you think it wants a good deal of nerve to brazen things out in the way that Todman did? I don't know about you, but if it had been me I should have turned tail at once."

"There's a lot in what you say, sir; but don't forget his old woman had sent him round to put his daughter in. Perhaps he was more frightened of her than what he was of you."

"There may be something in that, Sergeant," said Trimble, and he fell silent, mutely thanking heaven that he was not married to the unspeakable Mrs. Broome.

"Well, sir," the Sergeant went on, "that's two of them disposed of. Number three is Wendon, I suppose. He took her up to The Alps that afternoon, and he vanished just before she left, if young Ransome is to be relied on. After what Merrett has told us, it looks as if it might be a case of a lovers' tiff."

"We've no reason to think he was in love with her," the Superintendent objected. "Even the village only thought that he was after her money. If she refused him, killing her wouldn't make him any richer and wouldn't give him much satisfaction.

Besides, just because village gossip made a lucky shot in the matter of Mrs. Pink's money, it doesn't mean there was anything in the other story. All that we know about Wendon is that he was in her company fairly frequently and with her shortly before her death. If there's anything more to be known about him"—he swung the car off the main road into the West Yewbury lane— "now's the time to find out."

They were bumping over the rutted lane towards Horace Wendon's smallholding when Broome observed:

"You haven't mentioned your fourth suspect yet, sir."

"Oh, Sergeant, Sergeant," said Trimble reproachfully. "Do you mean to say that you have forgotten Humphrey Rose?"

"Rose, sir? But he wasn't there at the time."

"Was he not? How do we know? He was walking up from the station, remember. Todman had brought his luggage in the car. With Mrs. Pink walking down and Rose walking up I can't possibly leave him out."

"True enough, sir, when you put it that way. But I still don't see what Rose could have had to do with Mrs. Pink."

The Superintendent braked abruptly to avoid a hen that had blundered suddenly on to the lane. The car skidded in a muddy patch and came to rest under an unkempt hedge of flowering blackthorn, one wheel in a ditch.

"Damn!" he said quietly. "Now you'll have to push me out, I expect, Sergeant. But before you do, let me say a word about Humphrey Rose. I know of no conceivable connection between him and Mrs. Pink. I fancy that there is a pretty close one between him and Mrs. Ransome, though, and Mrs. Ransome knows more about the deceased lady than she's prepared to admit. Further, Rose has vanished very abruptly, and I got the impression that Mrs. Ransome was speaking the truth when she said that she didn't know where to. Further still, Rose is, I believe, one of the two or three wickedest men in England. So far as I know, he hasn't actually killed anybody yet with his own

118

hands, but I'm sure he'd not think twice about it if it suited him. Finally—but that's just a fancy of my own, and I propose to keep it to myself until we know a little more about the case."

A familiar look of deep depression had settled on the face of Sergeant Broome.

"Just when I was saying that this job was simmering down nicely!" he said.

"Quite. And now would you mind going to the back of the car and shoving when I give you the word?"

Quite himself again by now, Broome climbed wearily out and set his massive shoulder against the back panel of the car. One tremendous heave took it on to the track again, and a few minutes later the two officers drove into the filthy, litter-strewn yard of Wendon's homestead.

14

Mr. Wendon's Story

At first sight the place appeared to be deserted. Trimble gave the front-door bell a vigorous pull—the only effect of which was to establish quite conclusively that it was not in working order. He hammered loudly on the door and produced no response. It was only on walking round towards the back of the house that he met with the first sign of life, in the shape of an ill-conditioned terrier bitch which, from its appearance, had a family somewhere of much the same age as that of Marlene Banks. After a prolonged and suspicious inspection of the Superintendent's trouser legs it retreated a short distance and set up an ear-splitting succession of barks.

At the sound a door in a dilapidated range of sheds on the farther side of the yard opened to reveal the master of the house. He was carrying a roll of wire netting under one arm and a bundle of stakes under the other.

"Shut up, Phoebe!" he roared. The terrier scuttled off to some distant fastness behind the house, whence it continued to keep up a running commentary on the proceedings at the top of its voice.

"If you've come about pork," Wendon called across the yard to Trimble, "there's nothing doing."

"We haven't come about pork," Trimble shouted back. "We are police-officers, and——"

Wendon did not seem to have heard him above the clamour from Phoebe.

"I say there's nothing doing," he repeated. "In any case, I'm much too busy now."

He set off across the yard and away from the house. Sergeant Broome, who had remained by the car, cut him off.

"Just a moment, sir," he said. "This is a police matter, and we——"

"Police!" said Wendon with a disgusted air. "You seem to have nothing to do but persecute farmers. I've explained everything already to that Ministry of Food snooper, and he told me he was satisfied. What makes you think I've got any pork about the place?"

"This is nothing to do with pork, sir," the Sergeant repeated.

"I distinctly heard that man mention pork," Wendon persisted, indicating Trimble, who had now joined them, after picking his way across the muddy yard. "And if it isn't pork you've come about, I should like to know what it is."

"Mr. Wendon," said Trimble, "I am investigating the matter of the death of Mrs. Pink. I must ask you to be good enough to answer a few questions."

"I don't know anything about the death of Mrs. Pink," said Wendon shortly. "And I've told you already I'm busy."

"I am sure that you are not so busy that you can't give us a few moments, sir."

"It's all very well to talk like that, but people like you don't know what it is to try and run a smallholding single-handed. I'm not carrying these things about for fun, you know." He indicated the burdens in his arms. "If I don't get my chicken-run repaired pretty soon, I shall have the fowls all over the place before I know where I am."

"I expect it was one of your fowls we met just down the lane as we were coming here," the Superintendent remarked.

"Blast!" said Wendon peevishly, throwing his bundle down on to the ground. "That would happen, just when I thought I was going to get round to it at last! Did you happen to notice if it was a Leghorn? No, I suppose you wouldn't. Those fiendish birds will get out through anything. Oh well, I suppose I shall have to trust to luck that it'll have enough sense to come home to roost. It's too late to do anything about it now."

There was something almost pathetic, the Superintendent felt, in his readiness to admit defeat. He said:

"I just wanted to ask you a few questions, Mr. Wendon——"

"About Mrs. Pink—I know. Well, we'd better come indoors and get it over."

With a sudden access of energy he walked briskly ahead of them to the door of the house.

The room into which he showed them was of a piece with the exterior of the establishment—shabby, ill-cared for and untidy, a jumble of odds and ends cluttering up furniture that had once been good and was now fast falling into decay. He cleared two chairs for the officers by the simple process of dumping on to the floor the litter of books and papers that encumbered them, and then opened the door of a cupboard that stood in the corner of the room.

"I usually have a snifter about this time," he remarked, producing a bottle of whisky and a slightly dirty glass. "Would you care to join me?"

Trimble shook his head.

"Oh well!" Wendon poured himself out a generous helping. "Dash it! Where's the siphon? Excuse me a moment." He went out of the room, glass in hand, and returned almost at once with the whisky only fractionally diluted.

"Mrs. Pink," he said, and took a deep drink. "What do you want to know?"

"I think that she was an acquaintance of yours, sir?"

"Yes, I knew her. A very good sort of woman, Mrs. Pink. It was a shame she had to die like that." He appeared to be addressing his remarks to the glass in his hand rather than to the Superintendent. "A great shame, but there it was," he repeated.

"Would it be right to say that you were on friendly terms with her?"

"Well, yes, I don't mind admitting that. Friendly, certainly. Yes."

Down went the rest of the whisky at a gulp.

"There's no harm in being friendly with a woman, I suppose?" he said in a tone that started by being belligerent but diminished into a note of weak protest by the end of the sentence.

"It has been suggested to me that you might have been contemplating marriage to her," Trimble went on.

"Eh?" said Wendon in a startled voice. "Who said that?"

"I'm afraid I can't give you the source of my information, sir. The only question is whether it is correct or not." He paused, and added: "I am sorry to have to pry into your personal affairs like this, but you will understand that in a matter of this nature——"

"Oh, that's all right—I don't mind talking about it. It only beats me how a thing like that could have got about. I hadn't said a word about it to a soul. Not a soul—not even to her."

"You had not asked her to marry you?"

"No. It was just a passing idea that I had—that was all. Then I saw that it wouldn't do and I changed my mind. She wouldn't have had me, anyway. After all, who would?"

Wendon appeared to abandon the possibility of marriage to Mrs. Pink with the same air of peevish resignation that had marked his abandonment of the project of repairing his chicken-run.

"I see," said Trimble. "Now, knowing Mrs. Pink as you did, were you in any way acquainted with her private affairs?"

"She never said a word to me about them," said Wendon with emphasis.

123

"You knew, no doubt, that there was gossip in the village to the effect that she was a rich woman?"

Wendon shook his head.

"I don't belong to the village," he said shortly.

"It is a fact, sir, that she was extremely wealthy."

Wendon looked at the Superintendent directly for the first time since the interview began—looked at him for a long time, and in silence. When he spoke, it was only to say "Oh!" in a voice quite devoid of expression.

"That comes as a surprise to you, sir?"

"It does—absolutely. I thought she was hard up. Why, I even wanted her to sell something out of her house to raise a bit of money—she had some quite decent things, you know. She wouldn't do it, though. She said all her stuff had been her husband's, and I thought she was just a poor woman being sentimental. I had no idea...Have you found out yet who gets her money?"

"No, sir. We shall in due course, no doubt."

"Oh yes, obviously—of course you will. I was just wondering..."

"Now, sir," the Superintendent went on, "I want to ask you about the last time you saw Mrs. Pink alive. I understand that you drove her up to Mrs. Ransome's house on Thursday afternoon?"

"That's right. That Pettigrew fellow asked me if I'd do it, so I did. Just in the way of kindness, that was all. I mean, I hadn't arranged to do it, or anything of that sort. It was all on the spur of the moment, at Pettigrew's suggestion. I was going up that way in any case, and it just happened to fit in. Pettigrew will tell you that it was his idea, not mine at all."

"I have already seen Mr. Pettigrew, sir, and he confirms what you say."

"Oh—that's all right then. Only I didn't want you to think that just because I happened to run the lady up to The Alps that afternoon I had anything to do with—I mean that it was because of me that she went there, or anything of that sort. Because it wasn't, I assure you. It was a pure coincidence."

"You have made the position quite clear, sir."

"Good."

"Then, I think, having driven Mrs. Pink to The Alps, you drove down again?"

"That's right."

"By yourself?"

"Absolutely."

"I don't quite understand why you didn't give her a lift down the hill after taking her up there."

Wendon went rather red.

"That damned young prig of a boy at The Alps had the impertinence to ask her in to tea and leave me outside—that's why," he said. "Good Lord!" he added. "I've just thought. If she'd not gone in there she'd not have walked down the hill, and she might still have been alive today. It just shows, doesn't it?"

"According to young Mr. Ransome, you told him that you were going to wait outside the house till his mother came home. Did you?"

"No, as a matter of fact I didn't. I did hang about a bit, but I felt a bit silly, sitting there like a chauffeur while the quality had their meal indoors. I'm not a snob, sir—God knows, I can't afford to be—but there are limits, aren't there?"

"I see. You haven't told me yet, Mr. Wendon, why you went up to The Alps in the first place."

"It was nothing to do with pork," Wendon said instantly.

"Let's try to keep pork out of it, if we can."

"All right, then. It was just a small matter of a dozen eggs, if you want to know."

"You wanted to sell Mrs. Ransome some eggs?"

"That's right. Then, as she didn't turn up, I went round to the back and left them with that foreign woman of hers. Then I buzzed off."

"You came straight home?"

"Yes."

"You are sure you didn't stop on the way?"

"Stop on the way?" Wendon repeated. "I don't think so.... Wait a bit, though. Now I come to think of it, I did. My hand-brake was binding, so I pulled into the car-park off the road and attended to it."

"How long would that take you, do you suppose?"

"I couldn't say, exactly. It's a fiddling little job. Quarter of an hour—twenty minutes—perhaps more. I'm a rotten bad mechanic."

"I suppose you didn't look at your watch during that time?"

"No, I didn't. Actually, I haven't got a watch at the moment. I had to pop it the other day, if you really want to know. Does it matter?"

"It matters to this extent, Mr. Wendon. We believe that we can establish the exact time when Mrs. Pink arrived at the place where she met her death. One of the means of access to that place is a path leading down from the car-park——"

"Look here!" said Wendon, starting up. "What are you getting at?"

"Merely this—that if you were there at the appropriate time it seems possible that you might have seen or heard something that would help us."

"Oh, if that's all!" Wendon subsided into his chair again. "What is your approximate time, may I ask?"

"I see no harm in telling you—ten minutes past five."

"Then I shall have to work backwards. Let's see now...I was in here, listening to the six o'clock news. Before that I'd fed the chickens and shut them up—say ten minutes. Brewed myself a cup of tea—twenty minutes. That's half-past five, isn't it? Oh, yes, I'd forgotten—Phoebe had caught a rat in the meal store next to the pig-sty, and I wasted a good quarter of an hour trying to find where the hole was. Quarter past five, and allow ten minutes at least to get down from the hill, in second gear because of the state of my brakes—you see, I must have left at five past at the latest."

"Very well, we will assume for the moment that you left at five minutes past five. Did you pass anybody on your way down?"

"I can't say that I did. Not to remember, anyway."

"You are sure about that?"

"No, of course I'm not sure," said Wendon peevishly. "I've just told you as much, haven't I? How can you remember everybody you pass on the road? I wish you wouldn't pester me."

"I am sorry to pester you, as you put it, sir, but you must appreciate the possible importance of the question. Try to think, won't you?"

Wendon shook his head.

"It's no good trying," he said. "I can't remember. How was I to know it was important?"

"Nobody came past while you were attending to your hand-brake?"

"If they did, how was I to know? I had my head down, dealing with the job. I should have thought any fool could have seen that."

The Superintendent gave it up.

"We'll leave it at that, then," he said. "But if anything further comes to your mind you'll let me know, won't you?"

"Yes, of course I will. But I warn you, it won't. I haven't got that sort of memory."

"Very well. Now, if you don't mind, I'll put your statement into writing, and when you have signed it we shan't need to trouble you again."

"Just our luck, sir," said Broome with dismal relish on the way home, "getting a witness like that at the one place that mattered."

"What had you in mind, Sergeant?"

"Well, look. He must have met Todman's car going up, mustn't he? If the boy's right in his statement, Todman got to The Alps just when Mrs. Pink was leaving. It would take her just about five minutes to walk down to where Mr. Pettigrew lost sight of her. There's only one way up the hill, so the two cars must have passed. Yet he can't remember it."

"He wouldn't say positively that he didn't see anyone," Trimble reminded him, "merely that it didn't leave any impression on his mind."

"Nothing leaves any impression on his mind," said Broome bitterly. "Except pork. Either he's a complete nitwit, or he's trying to shield Todman."

"Can you suggest any reason why he should do that?"

"No, sir, I can't."

"Neither can I. There's another thing that occurs to me. If Todman left Rose at the bottom of the hill, why didn't Wendon see him walking up?"

"Same answer, sir, I suppose. Because he's the kind of fellow who doesn't see anything."

"There might be another reason for that, of course. There's only one road for cars up the hill, but several ways for people on foot. They are all of them in full view of the road, though, except one—and that's the way through the woods which Mrs. Pink was coming down."

"That just comes back to what I was saying, sir. If we could rely on Wendon the least little bit, his not seeing Rose would be important, perhaps. But when we know he didn't see someone who must have been there anyway, it proves just nothing, except that he can't be relied on. And what about Mrs. Ransome's car? Oughtn't he to have seen that too?"

The Superintendent shook his head.

"You forget," he said. "If the boy is right, she was at a lunch party at Didbury, on the other side of the hill. Mrs. Ransome approached the house from the other side. She only comes into the picture later."

128

"Of course," the Sergeant said a few minutes later, "Wendon's times may be all wrong. They're only guesswork, after all."

"Remarkably clever and fluent guesswork, at that, I thought. I'm wondering, Sergeant, if Mr. Wendon is quite so stupid as we think."

"He's remarkably stupid about the way he runs his holding," said Broome, who was himself country-bred. "Did you ever see such a mess in your life? I don't wonder he has to keep himself going with killing a pig every now and then on the sly. That reminds me, sir," he added, "did you happen to notice those stakes he was carrying when we first met him?"

"I did. Split chestnut palings. Old ones—bought second-hand, I expect, like the rest of the junk he had lying about the place."

"The weapon that killed Mrs. Pink, sir—what was that?"

"Split chestnut paling, too, but heavier. A corner post, I should say. But it's no good getting excited about that, Sergeant. You know as well as I do that half the fences in the county are made of that stuff. Mrs. Ransome's got a stack of old fencing posts just inside her front gate, I noticed. There are some posts missing from the fence between the Druids Hotel garden and the hill. I'm prepared to bet they're the same timber. Whoever hit Mrs. Pink on the head believed in using local produce—more's the pity."

Trimble had hardly re-entered his office when the telephone rang.

"Is that you, Mr. Trimble?" said a familiar voice. "I thought you might be interested to know that a kind friend in Scotland has sent me a very nice piece of salmon."

Even for Mr. MacWilliam it was an unorthodox opening. The Superintendent murmured, "That's very nice for you, I'm sure, sir," and waited to see what would come next.

"You'll come and help me eat it, won't you?" the Chief Constable went on. "Eight o'clock at my house."

"That's very kind indeed of you, sir," said the bewildered Trimble. He could not resist adding, "I'm, of course, very busy just now, sir, but——"

"We can do a little business after dinner, if you like. By the way, I shall have another guest."

"Indeed, sir?"

"A Mr. Paine. I think you might be glad to meet him."

"Mr.—who did you say, sir?"

"Paine. P for Percy. P also for Prufrock. P finally for Paine. In the middle of the vacation—did you ever hear the like? It looks as though you had lost the trip to London I promised you!"

With a final chuckle the Chief Constable rang off.

15

Paine's Fireworks

Mr. Paine was drinking sherry with the Chief Constable when Trimble arrived for dinner at the dark little house in the Cathedral Close. He was a large, fleshy man with a bald head and small, intelligent eyes.

The Superintendent never touched anything stronger than lemonade, and while the others finished their glasses he listened to Mr. Paine's description of the farm which he had recently bought just over the county boundary. Though his profession tied him to London, his heart, it appeared, really lay in the country. Particularly was he fond of Jersey cattle. He was also, the Superintendent noted, remarkably fond of the sound of his own voice, and the pre-prandial conversation was little more than a monologue. But of Mrs. Pink there was never a word.

They went into dinner, where Trimble listened without comprehension to a long, lyrical outburst provoked in Mr. Paine by a dark-red fluid which the Chief Constable poured for him out of a very dirty-looking bottle. When the salmon appeared it became immediately the theme for a spate of reminiscences. So far as Trimble could gather, Mr. Paine was even more knowledgeable on the subject of salmon than he was on those of Jersey cattle or the wines of France. Before the meal was over he had found occasion to air his learning on at least half a dozen other subjects, each of them quite unrelated to the others and equally unrelated to the only topic in which the Superintendent was interested. An awful suspicion crossed Trimble's mind. Had this talkative stranger disposed of his business in private with the Chief Constable already? Was he, the officer in charge of the case, being fobbed off with chatter and left to pick up the evidence, whatever it was, at second-hand? Under cover of a discourse on seventeenth-century Dutch flower paintings (of which Mr. Paine modestly remarked that he had the fourth best collection in private hands outside Holland) he stole a glance across the table and caught MacWilliam's eye. The look he saw there was wholly reassuring. The Chief, he could tell, had an entirely easy conscience. Something very like a wink travelled back over the debris of the dessert. That inscrutable connoisseur of human behaviour was enjoying himself at Mr. Paine's expense, in much the same way that he had known him to do at his—Trimble's—expense. Wherein exactly the enjoyment lay, the Superintendent, burning to get at the matter in hand, could not for the life of him tell, but he was satisfied.

They adjourned to the Chief Constable's study. Coffee for three; brandy for two; a cigar for one. MacWilliam filled his pipe. Trimble glowered in his usual self-imposed austerity. Mr. Paine stretched his legs out towards the fire, made a few erudite observations on the blends and brands of Cognac, and then observed:

"I am indebted to you for an admirable dinner, my dear Chief Constable. How very right you were to insist on not spoiling it by talking shop. People who speak of mixing business with pleasure simply don't know how to transact the one or to appreciate the other." He looked at his watch. "I shall have to be getting along directly," he went on. "It will take me at least three-quarters of an hour to reach home. I am running in a new car—a Fenwick Twenty. I don't suppose you have seen one yet? This is, I believe, the first of its design not for export. I think it is going to be remarkably good, though the suspension seems to me…"

For five minutes Mr. Paine analysed the Fenwick's suspension with an expert knowledge and enthusiasm that would have done credit to a working mechanic. Then he said:

"Well, as I say, I must be getting home. Before I go you'd like to know about Mrs. Pink, I expect?"

"Well," said the Chief Constable, with a perfectly straight face, "that was rather the idea, was it not, Superintendent?"

"Just so," said Mr. Paine complacently. "Luckily it won't take more than five minutes or so. Your conversation has been so enthralling that I've already stayed longer than I intended. I've been dealing with Mrs. Pink's affairs for a good many years now, and I think I may say that I have them at my finger-tips."

"What we principally want to know," said MacWilliam patiently, "is why this apparently penniless widow should turn out to be a wealthy woman."

Mr. Paine pursed his lips.

"Wealthy, ye-es," he remarked. "I suppose you might call her that. The estate will work out at about eighty thousand pounds, I suppose."

"Eighty thousand!"

"Approximately. Possibly more. I haven't the latest Stock Exchange quotations with me. There has been something of a fall in the capital values of one or two of her largest holdings recently, I am glad to say. Estate duties, as you are no doubt aware, are calculated on the prices ruling at the date of death. It is therefore sometimes quite important to expire at the right moment. But for practical purposes we can say eighty thousand. Six months ago the figure would have been higher. Comparatively wealthy, shall we say?"

"I'll say anything you like. But why should——"

Mr. Paine waved a plump hand.

"I recollect your question perfectly well," he said. "You need not trouble to repeat it. You are puzzled by the fortune possessed by this—ah—apparently penniless widow. Has it not occurred to

133

you, sir, that a simple explanation might be found in the fact that she was not only not penniless but also not a widow?"

Mr. Paine paused long enough for the Chief Constable to realize that some reply was expected from him.

"No," he said. "Frankly, that had not crossed my mind."

Mr. Paine shook his head in tolerant reproof.

"Surely, surely," he said, "you must be adequately familiar with the device by which assets of all sorts and kinds—often very substantial assets—are held by A for the use and benefit of B?"

"I've heard of trusts and that sort of thing, naturally."

"Trusts and that sort of thing, as you so compendiously put it, are what lawyers largely live by. We are not dealing here with a trust, in the strict legal sense of the word, but that is by the way. All that I am saying is that I am a little surprised that when a lady in the deceased's position is found to be in possession of a large estate it should not have at once been presumed that there was in the background a husband who, for reasons of his own, had elected to convey his property to her. It is the common process vulgarly known as 'putting it in the wife's name'."

"Then all this money," said the Superintendent, who could no longer keep silence, "is really Mr. Pink's."

"Oh no, no!" Mr. Paine was obviously shocked. "That would frustrate the whole purpose of the transaction. I have explained myself very badly if you have got that idea. The estate was—and had to be—exclusively, irrevocably, the property of the wife. She could do what she liked with it."

"Very well, then," Trimble persisted. "Why didn't she?" Mr. Paine looked at him with the air of a benevolent schoolmaster.

"I think I apprehend you," he said. "But your question is not quite accurately phrased. Mrs. Pink did, in fact, do what she liked with her property. The real problem is why she preferred to do what she did."

"Exactly," MacWilliam broke in. "We've all heard of the case of the apparently rich man who gets into difficulties and then, when his creditors come down on him, turns out to be quite penniless, because everything belongs to his wife. It's the oldest swindle in the world. But I've never before heard of its being worked in favour of a wife who wasn't even living with her husband, let alone a wife who was content to live in poverty. Unless you've explained that, you've explained nothing."

"That," said Mr. Paine, "is, if I may say so, a very proper and rational comment. The problem you raise is one that I have tried to resolve myself several times during the period in which I have been concerned with this lady's affairs. The solution, obviously, is one personal to her, and could only be finally given by someone who knew her far better than I. My personal acquaintance with her, I may say, was of the slightest, but I have my theory, and I think it is probably correct. Before I give it to you I should like to ask you a question. Would you say, from your enquiries, that Mrs. Pink was altogether normal?"

The Chief Constable smiled.

"Oddly enough," he said, "I put the very same question to one of her acquaintances only yesterday."

"Ah! And what answer did you get?"

"Yes and no."

"Did you find that answer particularly helpful?"

"In view of what I have learned this evening, I think that it was. My informant suggested that Mrs. Pink's abnormality—if you can call it that—consisted simply in the fact that she was an exceptionally good woman."

Mr. Paine nodded slowly.

"Yes," he murmured. "Yes. That is the only possible explanation. Not only exceptionally good, of course, but also more than ordinarily obstinate. And rather stupid as well. Isn't it lamentable, by the way, how often those three adjectives go together? There is your woman on the one side, and on the other a husband who not only had the wit to appreciate her qualities and to see what immense use they could be to him, but was also

135

prepared to gamble on them. For, mind you, he was taking a perfectly hair-raising risk. He must have known her uncommonly well before he did it—far better than most husbands know their wives, I fancy. After all, no normal woman would have put up with it for five minutes."

"You realize, I suppose," said MacWilliam, "that neither Mr. Trimble nor I have the least idea what you are driving at?"

"Haven't you? I'm sorry. I've been familiar with this odd situation so long that I was taking it for granted. Here's the story in a nutshell, then. Years ago, when they were first married, Pink formed the habit of giving his wife his savings to keep. She was thrifty and simple—and as we have agreed—good. He was extravagant and clever and—since we are passing moral judgments for once—bad. Not the kind of marriage to last very long, you'd say. This one didn't, as a marriage. But as a legal union it did. For one thing, Mrs. Pink was not the sort of woman who would ever consider divorce for a moment. For another, it suited Pink very well that it should continue. He knew her for a woman with an overdeveloped conscience, and he traded on his knowledge quite shamelessly. Long after they had parted, when he was moving in circles—I hesitate to say above—but far different from hers, he continued to transfer to her all the money that he could spare from his immediate needs, in the certain knowledge that with her obstinate sense of loyalty she would never touch a penny of it. Whenever he wanted it it was at his service. The Superintendent here said just now that this tidy little nest-egg was Mr. Pink's money, and of course I had to correct him. All the same, Mrs. Pink would have agreed with him. I explained the position to her time and again, but nothing would induce her to touch a penny of it. It was, in her eyes, his money, and when he wanted any he just came and took it. Fantastic, wasn't it? I know it's rude to call a lady a cow, but that's what she was—his milch cow."

Mr. Paine flicked the ash off his cigar and rose to his feet.

"Well, there you are," he said. "I think you know the whole

story now. Is it of any assistance to you in your enquiries, by the way?"

MacWilliam looked at Trimble.

"What do you say, Superintendent?" he asked.

"I rather think it is, sir," Trimble replied. "That is, if I'm right in an assumption that I've been making while Mr. Paine has been talking."

Mr. Paine looked at his watch again.

"I really must be getting along," he said. "What was your assumption?"

"That Mr. Pink changed his name after he left his wife."

"Oh, bless me, yes! I should have mentioned that. You are perfectly right—he did. That was many years ago, of course. She always refused to follow suit. I never quite comprehended her reason, but it was founded on some religious scruple or another. I know she quoted some text or another to justify it. If I can turn up the letter she wrote me on the subject I'll let you know what it was, in case you are interested."

"And that the name he took was Rose," Trimble went on, as Mr. Paine walked to the door.

"Naturally," said Mr. Paine over his shoulder. "From Pink to Rose was an obvious transition. Good night, my dear Chief Constable, and once more many thanks for your kind hospitality."

They followed him out into the hall. MacWilliam helped him on with his coat.

"Did she make a will leaving everything to him?" the Superintendent asked.

"Oh, Lord, yes," said Mr. Paine, reaching for his hat and gloves. "Every penny. What else would one expect?"

The Chief Constable held the door open for him, and he bustled out to where the resplendent new Fenwick Twenty was standing. Faint but pursuing, Trimble followed him.

"If Mrs. Pink was such a good woman," he said to Mr. Paine's broad back, "why was she prepared to help her husband defraud his creditors? Surely she must have known——"

137

Mr. Paine disappeared into the car. He pressed the self-starter and the engine sprang to life. Then he opened the window and thrust his head out.

"Sorry to run away like this," he said, "but if I don't get eight solid hours' sleep I'm done—absolutely done. I've got to be up early tomorrow to see my stockman, and I'm cutting it pretty fine. You are perfectly right about the creditors, of course, but, as I said, she was a very stupid woman in some ways. I don't think she can have ever properly understood what it was all about—not even when Rose was made bankrupt and went to jail." He switched on the lights and engaged the gear. "Actually, something seems to have opened her eyes just before her death, now you mention it," he added. "I had a letter from her on the subject only the other day. It may interest you. I'll send it on when I get back to the office. Good night!"

The car slid forward and gathered speed. Trimble watched the tail-light travelling round the Close until it disappeared beyond the cathedral. Now that Mr. Paine had gone it was suddenly, blissfully quiet.

16

A Walk After Church

"It's such a lovely day, Lady Furlong, I really prefer to walk," said Pettigrew. "Thank you very much all the same."

Morning service was just over at Yewbury Church. The size of the congregation augured well for the Vicar's Easter offertory. Pettigrew and his wife had just reached the lych-gate when Lady Furlong had approached them with an offer of a lift home.

"You'll come then, won't you, Eleanor?" said her ladyship. "I'm sure you abominate walking without cause as much as I do. Besides, it will give me a chance to talk about the Women's Institute. Things are really going to be rather difficult now that poor Mrs. Pink…"

With a look of bitter reproach at her husband Eleanor allowed herself to be led away to the car. Lady Furlong's offer had sounded too much like a command to be lightly refused. After being called "Eleanor" in front of the assembled worshippers of Yewbury, too! Pettigrew felt that his wife had received a public accolade. He wondered, as he saw them to the car, whether Eleanor would have the hardihood to call her formidable patroness "Prudence". It would have been almost worth while to have joined them to find out.

Once off the crowded main road Pettigrew thoroughly enjoyed his walk. He was in no particular hurry—Eleanor, he reflected guiltily, would be home in ample time to do everything necessary for lunch without his assistance—and he took a little frequented bridle-path that would lead him over the lower slopes of Yew Hill and back to the road again close to the Druids Hotel. He met a few determined-looking hikers and was over-taken by a string of unkempt hacks from the local riding-stables. Otherwise he had the path to himself, until, rounding a bend, he saw, walking in the same direction as himself, a slim young fig-ure that seemed familiar.

Pettigrew was walking at the sedate pace of an elderly gentle-man not in the best of condition, but he rapidly overhauled the boy in front. As he approached he remembered having seen him that morning, sitting in the pew in front of his own. It struck him, too, that for a boy of his age he was making very heavy weather of the gentle slope up which they were both moving. His gait was little better than a shamble, his shoulders sagged, and he wandered aimlessly from one side of the path to another. Like many another middle-aged man who had not been conspic-uously energetic in his youth, Pettigrew was inclined to be criti-cal of young fellows who did not hold themselves properly. "He'll be the better for his national service in a year or so's time," he reflected. "A good sergeant-major would have some-thing to say to him!"

Unconsciously he stiffened his own back as he drew level, and quickened his pace to an almost military step. The boy drew aside to let him pass and Pettigrew saw his face for the first time. The expression on it gave him quite a shock. He had seldom seen on anybody, of any age, a look of such utter dejection.

Pettigrew was a kind-hearted man, and his first instinct was to get away as quickly as he could and leave the sufferer to endure his private misery, whatever it was, without interference. But even as he took a pace forward he caught a glance that was unmistakably an appeal. The boy was not only miserable, he was

140

lonely. He paused in his stride, cursed himself for an incurable old sentimentalist, and then said in a hearty voice, "Morning! It's a lovely day, isn't it? Didn't I see you in church just now?"

"Yes," said the boy tonelessly. Then he pulled himself together with an obvious effort to be polite and added, "It's an interesting old church, don't you think? Do you know the brass in the Harvill Chapel?"

"I'm afraid not," said Pettigrew. "Brasses aren't much in my line. Are you interested in them?"

"Well, yes, I suppose so, in a sort of a way," said the boy with a woe-begone expression. He said no more for a moment, and Pettigrew was about to pass on when he spoke again.

"I say, sir—excuse me—but you are Mr. Pettigrew, aren't you?"

"Yes."

"I heard Colonel Sampson speaking to you after the service, that's how I knew."

"Oh, you know Colonel Sampson?"

"Not really. I've just met him, that's all. He's awfully decent, I thought."

"Yes. He's a very good fellow."

Another silence. Whatever it was that he wanted to say, it seemed to take a good deal of saying. They walked on steadily for a few more yards, and then—

"You are a judge or something, aren't you, sir?"

"Not a judge, actually, but I have been doing a little judging lately."

"I see. I was just wondering whether—I'm afraid you'll think it rather cheek on my part, but I was wondering——The fact is, I'm in rather a hole."

Oh Lord, thought Pettigrew, what is coming now? Avuncular advice is called for, obviously. Money, perhaps? Or has he got a girl into trouble? Whatever it is, it will be a confounded bore. Why didn't I take a lift in Lady Furlong's car when I could? Well, I'm in for it now.

141

"Suppose you begin by telling me who you are?" he said. "At the moment you have, as they say, the advantage of me."

"Oh, sorry; that was stupid of me. I ought to have said. My name's Ransome. My mother lives up at The Alps, you know."

"I see. I haven't had the pleasure of meeting your mother, but I know the house. I can just see the chimneys from my windows. Now that we are acquainted, what can I do for you?"

"It's awfully difficult to explain, really."

"So I perceive. I can only suggest that you tell me as shortly and crudely as possible what is troubling you. I'm not easily shocked, and if I can't help you I shan't hesitate to say so. What have you been up to?"

Pettigrew's calculated brusqueness had its desired effect. The boy flushed and said almost crossly, "I haven't been up to anything. If I had I shouldn't come to a perfect stranger for advice. This is a more or less public matter, and I thought you could tell me what I ought to do as a—as a citizen," he concluded, with a defiantly grown-up air that Pettigrew found irresistibly appealing.

"A public matter?" he echoed. "The only public matter I can think of that is likely to affect anyone at The Alps just now is the murder of Mrs. Pink. Is it anything to do with that, by any chance?"

"Yes, it is. How do you know?"

"Public matters are public knowledge, and, as I told you, I have a view of your chimneys from my house. Also I have a pair of field-glasses. Mrs. Pink had just left The Alps when she was killed. If you have any evidence to give about her you ought to be talking to the police and not to me."

"I have seen the police already. They took a statement from me yesterday."

"Very well, then, as a citizen you've nothing to worry about."

Godfrey sighed. "It's not quite as simple as that," he said. "You said just now you didn't know my mother?" he went on abruptly.

"Obviously not, or presumably I should have known you."

142

"That doesn't follow in my case, unfortunately. Till these holidays I hadn't seen her since I was a kid. She—er—she's rather an unusual sort of person in some ways."

"But what has your mother got to do——" Pettigrew stopped as a hideous thought crossed his mind. Was it possible that this wretched youth seriously thought that his own mother——? It would account for the misery that had first excited his sympathy, but—but what a grossly unfair position to put any man into, to expect him to advise in such a matter! he reflected angrily.

"Has your mother been asked for a statement by the police?" he asked.

"Oh yes. She wasn't terribly helpful, though."

"Well, that's her affair, after all. If you'd take my advice, I should simply leave the whole matter in the hands of the police, and not——" Not worry about it, he was about to say, but it seemed so patently foolish that the words died on his lips.

"I know," said Godfrey. "The trouble is, my mother is dreadfully silly in some ways, and I feel responsible for her."

The way in which he said it went some way to relieve Pettigrew of his worst fears.

"In what particular way is her silliness worrying you?" he asked.

"Well, she's got a friend who's been staying with us lately——"

"You mean Humphrey Rose?"

"Yes. Do you know him? I gather that he's fairly notorious."

"Notorious is the word." Pettigrew felt on safe ground at last. Until that moment he had quite failed to connect The Alps with the ex-convict whom he had last seen at Yewbury railway station. "Look here," he said, "I am, as you say, a complete stranger, and I still don't understand what you want my advice about. But I shall only give you the warning I should give to any son of mine if I had one. At all costs keep away from Rose. Even if it means leaving your mother's house—I gather that you are a fairly independent young man—get away from him, and keep away."

"Thanks very much," said Godfrey without any great enthusiasm. "As a matter of fact Rose has been rather nice to me——"

"He can be extremely nice when he wants to be. That's one of his most dangerous qualities."

"But the question doesn't arise at the moment, as he's left the house."

"Thank goodness for that!"

"And naturally the police want to know where he's gone to."

"I'm not sure that I follow that. We were talking about Mrs. Pink, weren't we?"

"That's just it. Rose came back to The Alps, walking up the hill just after Mrs. Pink left it, walking down. I told them that when I made my statement."

"I follow. Obviously they'd want to check up on him, as a matter of routine."

"Then he left the house in a hurry on Friday."

"What of it? It's a long way from that to prove any connection between that big City swindler and poor little Mrs. Pink. You've been imagining things, young man."

"There was a connection," said Godfrey soberly. "He called her Martha."

"Did he, by Jove! That must have surprised you. Tell me about it."

Godfrey related the incident of Mrs. Pink's bicycle accident. "And they went off together, like old friends," he concluded. "And he didn't come back till long after lunch."

"Interesting," said Pettigrew thoughtfully. "Interesting, and suggestive. Did you mention this to the police?"

"No. They didn't ask me anything about Mr. Rose except his movements on Thursday."

"I see. Well, if there really is any connection between them I expect the police are on to it by now. Was there anything else?"

"Yes. When he came back that afternoon he had a parcel with him. He showed it to me. It was a portrait of Henry Spicer."

"A cartoon by 'Spy', autographed by Spicer. I know. He presented it to the museum and got the local rag to write a paragraph about it."

"That's right. He told me he'd picked it up in the village, and of course I thought he'd bought it at the antique shop, but I remembered afterwards it was early-closing day. That must have come from Mrs. Pink's house."

"Very likely. It doesn't seem to me to be of much importance, but it all adds up. Rose doesn't seem to have been at much pains to disguise his acquaintance with Mrs. Pink from you, at any rate. But I don't see what this has to do with your mother being silly, or your duty as a citizen."

"Well," said Godfrey and became tongue-tied once more. "This is awfully difficult for me to say, but—my mother and Mr. Rose were——"

"Let's be men of the world and face it," said Pettigrew. "Living in sin, shall we say?"

"I'm afraid so."

"A very unfortunate predicament for you. I've already given you my advice so far as Rose is concerned, and that is quite independent of his relations with your mother. What follows?"

"Well, as I said just now, the police want to know where he is."

"And you know?"

"No, I don't. But I'm quite sure my mother does. She was telephoning to him last night, I'm certain, but of course I don't know where he was speaking from. Do you think I should——"

"Split to the police and let them make enquiries at the telephone exchange? M-m, you certainly have rather a problem there. On the whole, I think, No. It's most improbable that a man as well known as Rose will be able to remain hidden for any length of time—if he is hiding; and it's pure supposition that he is, at the moment. As for the other matter you mentioned, it might be of interest to them.... I tell you what, I have a certain acquaintance with some members of the local force. How would it be if I were to let them know that this information is available to them if they want it? Then, if necessary, you could slip down to the station and see them quietly without the

145

nuisance of having them crawling round the place again and putting you in an awkward position with your mother."

"I should be awfully grateful if you would, sir."

"That's a deal, then. And whatever you do, don't go wasting any sympathy on Rose. He is no good to you, and, if I may say so, he can't be any good to your mother. Is there anything else?"

They had reached the point where their paths diverged. Godfrey stood hesitantly for a moment, his eyes on the ground.

"I've been thinking," he said. "This connection between Mr. Rose and Mrs. Pink—what do you think it is?"

"Your guess is as good as mine, I should say."

"Do you suppose they could have been married?"

"It's a possibility, certainly, though it had never occurred to me."

"It only occurred to me last night when I was thinking things over. You know how it is when you can't sleep, sir?"

Pettigrew nodded. He knew well enough, but it gave him a pang to think that a boy of seventeen should.

"Suppose they were married," Godfrey went on, "and she wouldn't divorce him—she wouldn't, I know, she just wasn't that sort.... Well," Godfrey gulped hard, and then the words came out in a rush, "there are Mother and Mr. Rose in love with each other and everything, and—and it does add up to a motive, doesn't it, sir?"

So it's out at last! thought Pettigrew. He gave himself a little time before he spoke.

"Is your mother a rich woman?" he asked.

"Lord, no! She's always complaining about her overdraft."

"Where does her money come from, do you know?"

"Father made her an allowance while he was alive. It comes from solicitors now, I think. Then there is some money of her own—the trustees pay it every so often. She says it doesn't keep her in cigarettes. It comes to me when she dies, she said."

"Good! Then you have absolutely nothing to worry about on that score."

146

"You really think so, sir?"

"I'm quite positive. If there's one thing Rose would not be interested in, it would be marriage to a poor woman. You can put that right out of your head."

"I'm awfully glad to hear you say that, sir."

"Mind you," Pettigrew went on, "I'm not saying that Rose didn't murder Mrs. Pink. If it was worth his while he'd be capable of any sort of crime. But I'm quite sure, from what you tell me, that if he did, it was not because he was contemplating becoming your stepfather."

"I see. Do you—do you suppose my mother realizes that, sir?"

It took Pettigrew a little time to see what lay behind the question.

"Let's be perfectly frank about this," he said. "You were afraid that Rose might have murdered Mrs. Pink so as to marry your mother. That would be bad enough in all conscience, but what you're putting to me now is worse. You are toying with the theory that your mother might have done the same thing in the hope that Rose would marry her. Is that it?"

Godfrey had gone very red.

"It sounds horrible when you put it that way," he said. "Of course I don't really believe it—it's just——"

"It's just the result of a rather bad night and having nobody to talk it over with. To do a thing like that, for a motive like that, your mother would have to be both desperately wicked and extraordinarily stupid. Do you think she is that?"

"No. I don't."

"All right." Pettigrew looked at his watch. "I must be getting along," he said. "The roast lamb will be a cinder if I don't hurry up. I have only two more things to say: firstly, I'm very glad to have met you; and, secondly, that if you want to come and talk to me at any time I'm absolutely at your service. Don't forget! I really mean that."

They shook hands and parted. As Pettigrew went down the

147

path towards the road he looked back towards Godfrey, now striding up the slope towards Yew Hill. He was walking as a healthy lad should walk on a fine spring day, with the prospect of a good lunch in front of him. It was a heartening sight, and Pettigrew complacently told himself that he had done a good morning's work. But a little later, as he was urging his rather stiff legs up the lane on the other side of the valley, it occurred to him to wonder whether his confident assertions had been quite so convincing as they sounded at the time, and whether Godfrey's theory was not just the sort of one that a pigheaded policeman might seize on and run to—to death, perhaps?

17

Trimble v. Pettigrew

"Did you enjoy your walk?" asked Eleanor, as she and her husband finally sat down to a lunch that he remorsefully recognized as having been in the oven just a thought too long.

"Very much, thank you," said Pettigrew. "Did you enjoy your drive?"

"Yes. Lady Furlong was full of interesting talk."

"Mainly about Mrs. Pink, I suppose?"

"Mrs. Pink came into it, of course, but only incidentally. Lady Furlong is really more interested in the living than the dead."

"A very dangerous principle. The dead can't sue for defamation."

"Don't be unfair, Frank. You enjoy a good gossip as much as anyone. Her gossip isn't really malicious, anyhow. In fact, the only one of our neighbours she seems to have a down on is Mrs. Ransome. Did you know, by the way, that Mrs. Ransome has a son—a clever boy who was in church this morning?"

"Yes, indeed, I had the pleasure of his company on my walk. He's in rather a difficult position up at The Alps just now, and I've invited him to come in here whenever he feels inclined."

"Oh!" said Eleanor in a disappointed tone. "Then you won't want to hear about him. But I'm sure you didn't know that Colonel Sampson escaped from a prison camp in the first war and got home to find that his wife had run away with a conscientious objector."

"I remember hearing his divorce case tried. It made quite a stir at the time. They weren't quite so common then as now."

"Really, Frank, you are disgusting! If you know all these things, why do you keep them to yourself? I've a good mind not to tell you any more."

"Please go on. I can't possibly know anything about any of our other neighbours."

"Who else did she mention? Oh yes, Mr. Wendon."

"Not to disappoint you again, I've heard already that he was at Harrow with Lady Furlong's nephew."

"She knows a good deal more about him than that. It seems he was quite well off at one time. He went into some sort of business in the City and lost a tremendous lot of money."

"It depends what you call a tremendous lot. It was eight thousand three hundred and fourteen pounds."

"Frank!"

"Well, I'm sorry, but I could hardly help having that piece of information, seeing that Wendon gave it to me himself, on oath. At least that was the amount he said was owing to him, so I suppose it corresponds with what he lost. How he lost it he did not, of course, divulge. Did Lady Furlong tell you?"

"She said it was the Family Something-or-other."

"Not the Family Fundholdings?"

"That was the name."

"Good Lord!"

"Have I impressed you at last, Frank?"

"Well, yes, you have a little. It's just a coincidence, no doubt, but it's very odd how everything here seems to lead back to Humphrey Rose in one way or another."

"Rose? That's the man who the police believe may be able to assist them in their enquiries."

"Did Lady Furlong tell you that?"

"Of course not. She may be a gossip, but she does talk English. I thought you'd recognize the style. It was on the one o'clock news. I listened to it to while away the time waiting for you to come in from your walk."

The shaft went unheeded. Frank sat silently for a long while, his plate neglected, his nose furrowed with the wrinkles that were his characteristic sign of deep perplexity.

"Roses, roses all the way!" he murmured at last. Then he came out of his abstraction and finished his lunch in quick time.

"I shall do the washing-up," he announced firmly. "I want to work out a problem, and there is something about the rhythm of plate-drying that is conducive to thought."

"Haven't you finished your essay on torts yet?" his wife asked.

"I'm not considering torts at the moment. The study has shifted to crime—an allied subject, but very much less to my taste."

Trimble had had a bad morning. From an early hour he had been occupied with a mass of minor but essential business that had kept him tied to his desk until after midday. When finally he got away from Markhampton to renew his enquiries at Yewbury it was to meet with fresh disappointment. Mr. Todman, in apparent defiance of the urgent message which he had left for him the day before, was not at his home. Neither was Mrs. Todman. Even the garage hand had deserted his post at the petrol pump. A bottle of milk stood uncollected outside the front door of the house, and a Sunday newspaper was thrust halfway through the slit of the letter-box. Trimble's first instinct was to go to the policeman's cottage farther up the road, but he shrank from yet another encounter with Police-Constable Merrett. Instead he turned down the lane by the Huntsman's Inn and knocked on the door of the cottage that had once been Mrs. Pink's.

Marlene Banks came to the door at once.

"Oh!" she said with a start, on seeing Trimble. "I thought it was the police."

"It is," said Trimble, equally surprised.

He was about to go on to reel off his name and rank when Marlene said: "It is about Father?"

"Yes."

"Is he very bad?"

"Bad?" Trimble echoed in bewilderment. Then, looking at her pale, anxious face, he took in the situation at once.

"I wanted to see Mr. Todman," he said, "but he's not at home. Has he met with an accident?"

"Yes, I thought you'd know. Mr. Merrett brought us the news last night. A smash-up just outside Bognor yesterday—the car all to pieces, he said—an emergency operation, he said, and he'd let me know as soon as there was any news—Mother's in hospital too, only badly shocked, he said—the other poor chap what was on the motor-bike was killed outright, he said—Charlie's gone down there this morning, only I couldn't leave baby, of course—not having no telephone I can't get any news, but Mr. Merrett'll let me know as soon as there is anything, he said—the doctors were giving him blood fusion or something, he said, so of course when you said you was a policeman I thought…"

It took the Superintendent some time to get away from the distraught Mrs. Banks, and a good deal longer to establish over the telephone what the position really was. In the end the news that he was able to send back to the cottage was fairly reassuring to Mr. Todman's stepdaughter, though of small comfort to himself. Todman had had a narrow escape with his life, but would survive, in the absence of any unexpected complications, to face a charge of dangerous driving, if not worse. On the other hand, he would not be fit to be interviewed by a police-officer for some days at least.

If Trimble had not been so disappointed by his visit to Yewbury it would never have occurred to him to stop at Pettigrew's house on his way back to Markhampton. He had, in fact, a message for him, but it was scarcely one to justify a personal call from an officer of his rank. He did not expect to gain anything by it, and in spite of all Pettigrew's protestations he still regarded him with deep distrust as an intrusive amateur; but he was now in a mood for any line of action, however unpromising. The investigation, for the time being, was at a standstill, and being irritated by this supercilious lawyer was better than doing nothing.

Pettigrew was polishing the last of the plates when Eleanor announced the Superintendent's arrival. He went from the kitchen to the sitting-room, where he found Trimble inevitably staring out of the window at the hill opposite, now black with pleasure-seekers.

"Good afternoon," he said. "It's a nice view, isn't it?"

Trimble nodded.

"Is this where you saw Mrs. Pink on Thursday afternoon?" he asked.

"Yes. Let me lend you my field-glasses. Just where the yews start at the top of the hill. There's a man with a dog going down there now. Do you see him?"

Trimble focused the glasses in the direction that Pettigrew indicated and took a long look.

"Yes," he said rather grudgingly as he put the glasses down. "You could have seen her all right, just as you said. You didn't see anybody else on the hill at the same time?"

"No."

"Or just before or after?"

"No. I wasn't taking any particular notice of anyone else before, and there wasn't any after. I was called away just at the moment Mrs. Pink disappeared."

"In fact it was just a coincidence you happened to see her?"

"Just a coincidence."

"Pity," said Trimble shortly. He was silent for a moment or

153

two, and then went on, "I've a message for you from Mr. MacWilliam, sir. He asked me to let you know that the inquest will be on Tuesday at eleven, at the village hall in Yewbury. He would like you to be there if you can spare the time."

"Certainly I'll be there. If the coroner is going to take evidence I'll be prepared to do my stuff."

"It's for the coroner to decide, of course, but I expect the proceedings will be quite formal. In that case your evidence won't be wanted, but I'll see that a place is kept for you. We shall have a crowd, I should think."

"No doubt." Pettigrew looked inquisitively at his visitor. He seemed strangely reluctant to go, though his business was apparently at an end. "Is there anything else you wish to ask me?" he said.

"No, I don't think so, sir," said the Superintendent, but he still seemed to be waiting for something.

"There is one small matter I heard this morning that might be worth mentioning to you," said Pettigrew diffidently.

"And what might that be, sir?" asked Trimble sharply.

"I met young Godfrey Ransome today, and he——"

"I have already taken a statement from him."

"Quite. What he had to say did not relate to the day of the crime, but in view of the broadcast which you have just put out I thought it might be of interest, in case you chose to follow it up."

Pettigrew then repeated Godfrey's account of Mrs. Pink's bicycle accident and its sequel. Trimble listened to it impassively.

"Thank you, sir," he said ungraciously when it was over. "When I have the opportunity to interview Mr. Todman it will be interesting to have his version of the occurrence."

"Todman? Yes, of course. Actually, what concerned us—Ransome and me, I mean—was the apparent connection between Mrs. Pink and Rose."

Trimble pursed his lips. "Very likely it would," he said.

"You see," Pettigrew persisted, "the boy has a theory that possibly——But how silly of me! Of course you must know it already. Otherwise you wouldn't be hunting for him."

"Meaning, sir?"

"Meaning that Rose was Mrs. Pink's husband. After all, it's obvious when you come to think of it. Rose—pink—it stares one in the face."

"It's an extraordinary thing about this case," the Superintendent suddenly exploded, "that every damned thing that I find out through hard work and investigation along the proper lines turns out to be common knowledge already to all and sundry up and down the place. I find out that Mrs. Pink was a rich woman—then I'm told that that's been village gossip for years and years. I find out that she's married to this man Rose—and there's a schoolboy in front of me with the news. I suppose I was the last man in the county to hear that Todman smashed himself up in his car at Bognor yesterday. I don't know what people think's the use of a detective these days—I really don't. Simply laughing up their sleeves at one all the time, that's what they're doing. I expect, sir, you're simply bursting to tell me now who killed Mrs. Pink and how and why he did it. All I can say is, I don't want to hear it. Not now I don't. When I've finished the case and made the arrest and seen the man tried and convicted, then you can come along if you like and tell me you knew it all the time. Till then I should be much obliged if you'd leave criminal investigation to those whose duty it is to do it!"

Eleanor came into the room a few minutes afterwards to find her husband sitting back in an armchair, helpless with laughter.

"What on earth have you found so funny?" she asked.

"Detective-Superintendent Trimble of the Markshire County Constabulary," spluttered Pettigrew.

"He always struck me as rather a serious sort of man."

"He is funny because he is so serious. Also he is rather pathetic. It's cruel to laugh at him, really."

"What did he come to see you about?"

"That is part of the joke, as a matter of fact. He came, nominally, to tell me that Mrs. Pink's inquest is fixed for Tuesday. Actually, whether he knows it or not, it was for the express purpose of losing his temper with me. It took him a long time to manage, because I didn't give him a fair opportunity, but he did it at last, and now he's gone away feeling ever so much better. It was quite a spectacle."

"But why should he want to lose his temper with you particularly?"

"He had to blow off somehow. The poor chap is obviously in a state of dither. What with Rose having disappeared and Todman in hospital, his two prize suspects are out of his reach, and he's suffering from an acute sense of frustration. As to why he chose me, that sticks out a mile. You see, in spite of all my endeavours to be a good boy and keep my nose out of what doesn't concern me, I'm still public enemy No. 1 so far as he's concerned. I'm the wicked amateur who wants to go behind his back and teach him his business. He accused me just now in so many words of wanting to tell him who murdered Mrs. Pink."

"How absurd, Frank! As if you could possibly know!"

"Come to think of it," said Pettigrew, suddenly serious, "I do."

18

Trimble v. Rose
(Wendon Intervening)

The inquest was held in the village hall at Yewbury. The coroner
sat at a table on the platform at the end of the hall; to the one
side of him a row of self-conscious jurors, to the other an impressive selection of press representatives. It was an appropriate set-
ting, for it was there that Mrs. Pink had so often figured, a quiet,
unobtrusive but essential personage on every committee,
prompting the chairmen of innumerable meetings with answers
to awkward questions, reading the minutes of proceedings of
every sort of parochial society, modestly acknowledging the
inevitable tribute to her valuable work behind the scenes of this,
that or the other activity. It seemed quite unnatural to the villagers who packed the body of the hall that Mrs. Pink was not
present in person to see that everything was in order.

Apart from the inevitable absence of the subject of the inquiry,
nothing was lacking to make up a village occasion on the grand
scale. Every resident who could possibly be squeezed into the
building was there, and most of them had been patiently waiting
for the proceedings to begin for an hour or more before Pettigrew slipped into the seat which the Chief Constable, as good as

his word, had reserved for him. The crowds of disappointed late-comers whom he had seen turned away at the doors were, he noticed, mostly composed of strangers. That was as it should be. This was, after all, a local show. It was a pity, he reflected, that it was going to be so dull and so brief. There was still a glamour about the name of coroner's courts, but their great days were over. He passed the time of waiting in trying to recollect exactly when it was that Parliament had relieved coroners from the task of amateurishly duplicating the work of the magistrates and police. He could not remember. It did not matter. Nothing of the smallest interest was going to happen today, at all events, and he could not for the life of him say why he had come there himself, except that, having finished the lecture on torts, he was at a loose end that morning, and that sitting with his neighbours in the village hall made a change from pottering round the garden at home.

He glanced around him, picking up here and there a familiar face in the throng. He threw what he hoped was an encouraging smile in the direction of Godfrey Ransome, who had come into a reserved seat a little distance from his own, and then occupied himself in the always fascinating task of trying to read his neighbour's newspaper without too obviously drawing the attention of the owner. The headline was clear enough: WHERE IS HUMPHREY ROSE? was spread clean across the top of the front page. A blurry patch below and to one side was presumably a photograph, but the light was poor, and he had to take it on trust. By squinting vigorously he could just decipher part of a passage in leaded type. Needless to say, it resolved itself into "… believe may be able to help them in their inquiries".

He was still absorbed in this childish game when he became aware that the inquest had begun and the jury was already being sworn. Stumbling over the unaccustomed words, in a ragged chorus they promised that they would diligently enquire and true presentment make, and so on to the end of the time-honoured formula, just as though they really had a useful function to perform.

The coroner, contrary to all tradition, proved to be a quiet young man with a modest, almost shy, demeanour. In a voice barely audible beyond the first few rows of chairs, he informed the jury that he proposed to lay before them evidence of the identity of the deceased and then to adjourn the proceedings. Whether they would be summoned again would depend upon the result of the investigations then being conducted by the police. He called Police-Constable Merrett.

Taking the centre of the floor with measured tread, Merrett held the Testament aloft and recited the oath in ringing tones. At nine o'clock that morning, he announced, he had proceeded to the mortuary of the Royal Markshire Hospital at Markhampton and had there seen the body of——

"Excuse me, Mr. Coroner, but may I say a word?"

A deep, cultured voice from the back of the hall interrupted the proceedings. Merrett stopped his evidence midway, the heads of the audience turned from the direction of the platform towards the entrance behind them, and there was a momentary hush. Pettigrew, who, like many people, had never heard but often secretly longed to hear a stranger forbid the banns in church, felt that he was witnessing the nearest approach to it that he was ever likely to experience. Looking behind him, he could see some sort of a scuffle going on near the door, where apparently the interrupter was trying to force his way further in.

"There must be silence!" said the coroner, with an unexpected rasp to his voice. "If there is any further disturbance I shall order the court to be cleared." He motioned to Merrett. "Proceed," he said.

But Merrett did not proceed. From his vantage-point on the platform he was looking down into the hall with an air of bewilderment on his broad, honest face. He turned to say something aside to the coroner, and as he did so the voice spoke again.

"I have a right to be heard," it said, "and I insist upon being heard. Let me pass, please."

A moment later Humphrey Rose, slightly dishevelled from his struggle with the doorkeeper, but otherwise perfectly self-possessed, walked up the hall. He was nattily dressed in a dove-grey suit, to which he had very properly added a black tie.

"Mr. Coroner," he said, "I must apologize for this intrusion, but am I not correct in thinking that it is usual for evidence of identification at proceedings of this nature to be given by the next of kin? If so, as husband of the deceased I feel that I should be called upon rather than this witness."

The coroner, Pettigrew was glad to observe, was entirely equal to the occasion.

"May I ask, sir," he said calmly, "whether you have seen the body of the deceased?"

"To my regret, no. I have come from some distance and have not yet had the opportunity."

"Then you are not qualified as a witness."

Rose smiled amiably. "I am ashamed to say that I had over-looked that all-important point," he said. "Would it be possible for the proceedings to be adjourned so that I could qualify?"

"Certainly not."

"I am in your hands, sir. In that case I have nothing further to say, except to ask you once more to accept my apologies."

And that, as Pettigrew recollected afterwards with mild astonishment, was the end of the whole extraordinary episode. Merrett resumed his evidence, his deposition was laboriously written down and signed, and the inquest was formally adjourned. The appearances were beautifully preserved. So far as the record went, there had been no more than a minor inter-ruption, lasting a bare two minutes, which had been dealt with by the court in the only proper way. Up to the end of the brief session nobody in the assembly behaved as though anything in the least out of the way had occurred. It was an extraordinary example of English calm—or should one call it sluggishness?—in the face of the unexpected.

The coroner announced the adjournment, gathered up his papers and left the hall, followed by the officials present. The public stood respectfully until they had gone. There was a short moment of indecision, a scraping of chairs and benches on the wooden floor as people gathered up hats and coats and hand-bags, and then a low murmur of talk, pitched in that toneless semi-whisper in which the inhabitants of Yewbury prefer to converse with one another in public places. They had, every man and woman of them, just experienced the greatest thrill of their lives, but nobody would have guessed it from their demeanour. Very slowly and quietly they began to file out, hampered in their progress towards the door by the pressmen, who, the only persons present uninhibited by village manners, had dashed from the platform and followed as close as they could upon the heels of the coroner and his little procession.

It was not the coroner they were after, of course. The last of the group for which the village courteously made way was Police-Constable Merrett, whose broad back effectually blocked any attempt to pass him in the narrow gangway between the seats. Two in front of him and immediately behind the coroner went the Chief Constable. And sandwiched between the Chief Constable and Merrett, walking close together like old friends, were Detective-Superintendent Trimble and Humphrey Rose. The whole thing had been done so quietly, so naturally, that it might have been rehearsed. By the time the first eager reporter had reached the road outside, the door had already closed on the waiting police-car. In the words that were to be read at five million breakfast tables next morning, Mr. Rose had been invited to accompany police-officers to the station—and Mr. Rose had elected to avail himself of the invitation.

Pettigrew found himself jostling Godfrey in the slowly moving progress out of the hall.

"I think this has solved your problems," he murmured to him.

The boy nodded. Then he said gloomily, "In a way, sir, yes. But don't you think it has perhaps raised some others?'

Pettigrew gave himself time to think that over. When they were outside he turned to Godfrey and said with an air of crisp decision:

"My immediate problem is that I have a lawn urgently in need of mowing and a mass of weeds to remove from the herbaceous border. It is always easy to prescribe for others, but I suggest that the best thing for you at the moment is a spell of hard, physical work. I can offer you that, if you care to come up to my place now, with a bite of lunch and as much drink as you can carry thrown in. What do you say?"

"Thank you, sir. I'll come."

They set off together, picking their way with difficulty past the knots of eagerly gossiping villagers. It was not difficult to tell from the snatches of talk which they overheard what was the general reaction to the morning's events. The duplicity of Mrs. Pink in having concealed the existence of a husband was enthusiastically condemned by one and all. She was variously described as sly, deceitful, and even—ultimate reproach—as no better than she should be. As for her death, she had got what was coming to her and no mistake, and such expressions of sympathy as made themselves heard were reserved for the poor fellow who they wouldn't even let see his own wife's corpse when he asked to.

On the last point, at least, the village did the authorities an injustice. As the police-car drove into Markhampton Rose broke the silence which he had maintained up to that point by asking with his usual genial politeness whether it would be convenient to stop at the mortuary on the way to the police-station. Permission was granted, and the car was diverted accordingly. Arrived at the hospital, Rose threw away the stub of the cigar which, to Trimble's intense discomfort, he had been smoking all the way

162

from Yewbury and went with the Superintendent into the building. Five minutes later they returned. In suitably grave tones he discussed and approved the arrangements that had been made for the funeral, then lighted a fresh cigar and announced jauntily that he was at the Superintendent's service.

"Let me get one thing clear at the outset," he began, when he was finally installed in Trimble's office. "I am not under arrest?"

"Certainly not, sir."

"Very well. It follows that I am here entirely of my own free will?"

"Yes, sir."

"I should be glad if that could be put upon record. As an ex-convict I value my personal liberty rather more than most men. Now, how can I help you?"

"We will begin at the beginning, if you don't mind. Your name is Humphrey Rose?"

"I think you know the answer to that one. Yes."

"Your address?"

"I hesitate to say that I am of no fixed abode, Superintendent, because the expression has rather degrading associations. I have booked a room at the Druids Hotel for the next few days. Will that do?"

"You were staying until recently at The Alps?"

"Quite right."

"I will come back to that later. Now I understand you to say that you are the husband of the deceased?"

"Yes. To make the position quite clear, I have here my marriage certificate and a copy of the deed-poll by which I changed my name. I suppose, by the way, that my little announcement at the inquest this morning did not come as a surprise to you?"

"I am not here to answer your questions, Mr. Rose. When did you last see your wife?"

"A week or two ago. I forget the exact date. We met accidentally in the road. She had fallen off her bicycle and I took her back to her house."

163

"Was that the occasion when you took from her a portrait which she had there?"

"The 'Spy' cartoon of Spicer, you mean? Quite right. No doubt you read of my presenting it to the local museum afterwards? It seemed a harmless piece of vanity at the time, but I wish now I hadn't done it."

"What do you mean?"

"Well ..." Rose extended his hands. "You will have to work that one out for yourselves, I am afraid, but I have a notion that it had unfortunate consequences. You were saying——?"

"Was that the last time you saw your wife?"

"Until this morning—yes."

"I want to come to last Thursday, the day on which the murder took place. You were staying at The Alps at the time?"

"Yes. That was my headquarters. I spent Wednesday night in London, though. I had business appointments there on Thursday morning. Do you want to know what they were?"

"I am interested in what occurred after you returned from London. You came down by the train due at Yewbury at four thirty-five, which on that evening was running six minutes late?"

"I wasn't aware that the train was late, but no doubt your information on that point is accurate."

"You were met by Todman's car, but decided to walk, leaving him to take up your luggage?"

"That is nearly correct. Actually I let him drive me to the foot of the hill and put me down there. I don't care for walking on roads."

"What time did you reach The Alps?"

Rose considered for a moment. "It's difficult to say exactly," he said. "It was after a quarter past five, I should think. Say twenty past and you won't be far wrong. I'm a slow walker."

"Very slow, if it took you as long as that," Trimble pointed out. "Did you stop on the way?"

"I expect so. To look at the view and get my breath and so on."

"There are several paths up the hill. Which one did you take?"

164

"The easiest one, naturally."

"Not the most direct route, through the trees?"

"Certainly not."

"Very well. You say you took the easiest path. That is the one that follows the main slope of the hill. Did you meet anybody on the way?"

Rose did not reply for some time. Then, in a hesitant manner, and in marked contrast to his fluency up to then, he said, "I really can't remember."

"Do you really mean that, Mr. Rose? Think. It may be important."

"I was taking no particular notice. I may have met someone or I may not. It is really impossible to say."

"If you were where you say, you were within view of the road near the top of the hill. Was there any traffic going up or down?"

"I rather think I saw a car going down—possibly more than one. I can't be sure."

"It comes to this, then, that there is nothing but your word to show that you were on the path you describe at, shall we say, ten minutes past five, and not in the yew trees on the opposite slope of the hill?"

"I don't quite know what is the significance of ten minutes past five," said Rose easily, "though I could hazard a guess. But you must take my statement—which, I would remind you, is a purely voluntary one, made without pressure or threat and without my having been cautioned—for what it is worth. Any comments you choose to make upon it are your affair."

Trimble changed the subject abruptly.

"Would you care to tell me," he said, "where you went to on Friday?"

"Actually," said Rose, "I should. I went away on business to a rather remote spot in the North of England. I don't propose to give you any further details."

"On business, Mr. Rose? Over the Easter holiday?"

"And when do you suppose, sir," Rose rejoined in a contemptuous tone, "that business is done? I'm speaking of business that matters, involving important people and important interests—things that you wouldn't begin to understand. It's done, of course, when offices are closed, and when the people who really matter can get together and discuss their affairs without interruption. I do not propose to tell you anything about it or to disclose the names of my associates. This whole affair has probably done my projects irreparable harm as it is. As soon as I was aware of what had occurred I came back in order to give you what assistance I could. And all the thanks I get for it is to be accused—not in so many words, I grant you, you are too clever for that—but virtually accused of murdering my wife. As if any man of sense couldn't see the absurdity of such a proposition to a man in my position!"

Then Trimble played his trump card.

"When you speak of a man in your position," he said softly, "you mean an undischarged bankrupt with all his property in his wife's name?"

"That is not a correct way of putting it. I am—was, I should say—a man with no property whatever, and a wife who had a good deal."

"A wife, at all events, who was quite prepared to let her husband deal with the money exactly as though it was his own?"

"A wife who chose to be generous with her property towards her husband."

"Suppose, Mr. Rose, the wife had changed her mind and chose to apply the money in her hands to paying some of the bankrupt's creditors? That might change her value in the eyes of her husband, might it not?"

"What the devil do you mean?"

"I mean that your wife, three days before her death, wrote to her solicitor, saying that she had just realized the hardship which your bankruptcy had imposed on many people, and on one in particular, and enquiring what securities he suggested she should sell so that she could make an immediate payment of eight thousand odd pounds, with more to follow. Does that come as a surprise to you?"

166

Rose did not answer the question. Instead he muttered in a low, angry voice, "I should like to see that letter."

"It will be produced in due course. I have not got it, but it was read to me over the telephone this morning by the person to whom it was addressed. Have you anything further to say about it, Mr. Rose?"

Rose's pale cheeks had assumed an almost greenish hue. Somehow he mustered a smile. "It makes quite a difference, doesn't it?" he said. Then he stood up. "Unless there are any further matters on which you wish to question me," he went on, "I should like to go."

"You are a free agent, sir," said the Superintendent ungraciously. "But I should like to know where you are going."

"I have given you my address already—the Druids Hotel."

"In that case, if you have no objection to waiting a few moments, I will arrange for a car to take you there."

"That arrangement would suit both our purposes very well, I fancy," said Rose calmly. He had by now to some degree recovered his poise. "I hope you will not keep me waiting long. I am beginning to feel in need of my lunch."

"No. I will see that you are back in good time for your lunch."

Trimble rang a bell on his desk and said to the officer who answered it, "Show this gentleman to the waiting-room and order a car for him as soon as possible."

The officer saluted and then murmured something in the Superintendent's ear.

"Is he?" said Trimble. "Then show him in at once."

"Very good, sir."

The officer left the room, and Rose followed him to what the Superintendent was pleased to call the waiting-room. The headquarters of the Markshire Constabulary, like most police buildings, were old, and hopelessly out of date for the purposes which modern conditions had imposed upon them. Even if they had not been largely reduced in usable area by a direct hit during the war, they would have been far too small for comfort or efficiency. As it was, the one and only place where callers could be deposited was little more than a large, lighted cupboard, partitioned off from the main C.I.D. office. It was disagreeably reminiscent of a cell.

Rose's guide flung open the door of this dismal apartment and said to him, "Will you wait in here, please?" and in the same breath to somebody inside, "The Superintendent will see you now, sir." The incoming and outgoing inmates met face to face.

"Well!" said Rose, his face wreathed in smiles, "if it isn't my old friend Wendon!"

"Get out of my way, you filthy bastard!" said Horace Wendon.

Detective-Sergeant Broome, who was gloomily arranging a file of papers in the office, looked up with interest and made a note of the encounter.

"Well, Mr. Wendon?" said Trimble.

Wendon was obviously in a state of some excitement. It had the effect of reducing him almost to incoherence, and it was some time before any words came.

At last he stammered out, "Look here, you're making a ghastly mistake."

"What do you mean, exactly?"

"Arresting Rose, I mean. You're absolutely barking up the wrong tree."

"And who told you that I had arrested Mr. Rose?"

"Damn it, I was at the inquest this morning—I saw you do it. And it's absolutely wrong, I tell you. The man may be the biggest swine on earth, but I'm not going to stand by and see him hanged for a crime he didn't commit, whatever else he may have done. It's not cricket."

"Now, calm yourself, sir. Take things easy and we shall get on a lot better. Nobody has been arrested yet. Mr. Rose has come here at my invitation to answer a few questions and make a statement, just as you made a statement. That is all. You've got no business to jump to conclusions and talk about innocent people being hanged, or nonsense of that kind."

"But it said in the paper——"

"If you believe everything you read in the papers at your time of life, Mr. Wendon, you must be a very simple man. In any case, what it said in the paper was that we were looking for Mr. Rose. So we were. Now we have found him. Whether he or anybody else is arrested remains to be seen."

"But you may arrest him—that's the point. And I happen to know that he is innocent."

"Do you, indeed, Mr. Wendon? And how, may I ask?"

"That's what I'm trying to tell you. When I saw you the other day you told me to come back and let you know if I remembered anything further."

"I recollect that perfectly well. I recollect also that you said it wouldn't be any use, because you hadn't that sort of memory."

"Well, I have remembered, and it was seeing Rose at the inquest that reminded me."

"Reminded you of what?"

"Reminded me that I saw Rose on the hill on Thursday afternoon."

"What was he doing?"

"He was walking," said Wendon, speaking now very deliberately and carefully, "he was walking up the hill by the main path over the slope. I was fiddling with my car on the road, as I told you, and I saw him coming from a long way off. Then I started up and came down very slowly, because of my brakes. I had him in view pretty nearly the whole way, and he kept on straight to the brow of the hill. He was nowhere near the trees all the way."

"You seem very positive about it, Mr. Wendon."

"I *am* positive. Damn it all, you needn't think I'm making this up to save the skin of a filthy little rat like Rose. It's simply that I'm not going to stand by and see an innocent man——"

"Yes, you've said that before. It's a pity you couldn't remember this important piece of evidence when I saw you on Saturday."

"Well, I'm sorry, but that's the way my memory works. It just wants a bit of jogging, and seeing you taking Rose off after the inquest gave it the jog. That was all."

"Very well." Trimble sighed. He looked suddenly very tired. "I'll have what you have said put into statement form, Mr. Wendon, and when you have signed it you can go."

He went out of the room for a moment. In the office outside he signalled to Sergeant Broome.

"Has Rose left yet?" he asked him.

Broome looked out of the window.

"Just getting into the car, sir."

"Run down and stop him, will you? I must see him again after Wendon has gone. Then send a typist to my room."

When Wendon had departed Rose was brought back into the Superintendent's room. This time the interview was very brief.

"Just one more question, Mr. Rose. You spoke of seeing a car going down the hill. Can you describe it?"

"Yes," said Rose without hesitation. "It was one of those jeep affairs with a snub nose."

"So that," said Trimble afterwards to Broome, "is that. If Wendon is telling the truth about that odd memory of his, Rose is clean out of it."

"And why shouldn't he be telling the truth, sir? If ever a man hated another like poison, he does Rose. You should have seen him when they met in the waiting-room just now."

"And Rose, on his side, has just presented Wendon with a perfectly good alibi. I don't somehow see him doing that sort of thing out of pure kindness to his fellow man." The Superintendent shrugged his shoulders. "Is there any further news from Bognor yet?" he asked abruptly.

"Not yet, sir."

"Ring up the hospital and find out if Todman will be fit to be seen tomorrow. Tell them it's urgent."

Urgent—Urgent. The word beat like a drum in Trimble's head as he went back to his desk, to read once more his ever-growing file which sooner or later, with all its gaps and defects, would have to be proffered for inspection by the kindly but alarming eyes of his Chief Constable.

19

The Hospital and the Hotel

The ward sister said, "You can see Mr. Todman now. But please understand that he is to be kept very quiet. And you are not to stay too long. When I tell you that you're to go, you'll go, and no nonsense about it. Is that understood?"

She was a tiny little woman with red hair and a thin, hard mouth. The two large detectives quailed before her. Meekly they assured her that they understood perfectly. Meekly they followed her down echoing, hygienic passages to Mr. Todman's bedside.

From beneath a mass of bandages a pair of cold grey eyes stared balefully up into Trimble's face.

"So it's you again, is it? I might ha' known," said Jesse Todman.

"I'm not going to worry you for long," said the Superintendent in a reassuring tone. "Just a few questions——"

"You can keep your questions, mister, and I'll tell you straight. That cyclist never gave a signal. I don't care what anyone says. Never a sign of a signal. How was I to tell he was going to turn?"

"I'm not concerned with the cyclist, Mr. Todman. The Sergeant here and I are only interested in the case of Mrs. Pink."

"Perishing old bitch!" said Mr. Todman. He closed his eyes, and for a moment it seemed as though that was his final comment on Mrs. Pink. Then he looked up again, and this time there was an expression of fear in what could be seen of his face.

"'Ere!" he said. "Have you been on at my Marlene again over that house of mine?"

"It's nothing to do with the house this time, Mr. Todman."

"That's all right, then. So long as Marlene's comfortable I don't care what happens to me. Mrs. Pink! Ha! That was a turn-up and no mistake. I wrote and warned her, but it wasn't no use. If she'd got out when I told her to, maybe all this would never have happened. Three hundred pounds I offered her and she wouldn't see reason. And if she'd waited to listen to me I'd have made it four fifty. But would she stop when I called to her? No. There she went, with four hundred and fifty pounds behind her and sudden death in front. That's a judgment, if ever there was one, eh, mister?"

"Where did she go, Mr. Todman?"

"Down the hill, of course, down the Glade—*you* know."

"And you went after her?" said Trimble softly.

At first it seemed that Todman had not heard him. He had closed his eyes again, and now leaned back on his pillow, apparently exhausted by his effort. The sister, standing at the head of the bed, turned towards the Superintendent and drew breath to speak. Then, quite suddenly, Todman came to life again, and this time there was an unexpected malicious grin on his face.

"I could 'ave, couldn't I?" he said. "I know what you're getting at, mister—you can't fool me. But I didn't. Just sat there in the car like an idiot, cussing and swearing to myself, for I don't know how long—five, ten minutes perhaps. I never so much as set foot on the path. Ask Mrs. Ransome if I did."

"Oh! Mrs. Ransome saw you there, did she?"

"I'm not saying she did. All I'm telling you is she would have seen me if I had. See?"

"Would have seen you? Why?"

"'Cause I should have walked on top of her, of course," said Todman impatiently. "That path only leads one way, s'far as I know."

"Let's get this quite clear," said Trimble as calmly as he could. "You saw Mrs. Ransome going down the path—with Mrs. Pink?"

"Not with her—after her."

"How long after her?"

"How should I know? A tidy time, I suppose. Not so long, either. Say a couple o' minutes, more or less."

"Was she walking fast or slow?"

"Oh, she was hurrying all right. Fast enough to catch that fat old cow up if she'd wanted to."

"Had she anything in her hand? A stick or anything?"

"I didn't take that much notice."

"And you didn't see her come back?"

Todman shook his head.

The sister had her hand on Todman's pulse. She frowned slightly. "I think——" she said.

"Just a few more moments, madam, please," Trimble begged. "We shan't be long now, I promise you. Mr. Todman," he went on hastily, "after you had seen Mrs. Ransome go down the path, what did you do?"

"Went home."

"Now I want you to think very carefully, because it may be important. Did you see anybody on the hill as you came down it?"

"No."

"Nobody at all?"

"Nobody—except Mr. Rose, of course."

"I don't know why you say 'of course', Mr. Todman."

"'Cause I'd left him at the bottom to walk up, that's why. It stands to reason he'd be coming up when I was coming down, don't it?"

"Where did you see him?"

"On the brow of the hill. I was taking the corner on the other side of the valley, like, and I looks across and sees him."

"And you saw nobody else?"

"I've told you that already."

"Did you see Mr. Wendon's car?"

"Yes, I saw that."

Todman's speech was becoming ominously feeble. It was a question, Trimble felt, whether he had already reached the stage when he was prepared to agree to any suggestion put to him from sheer lassitude. Fighting against time, and desperately avoiding the sister's eye, he put another leading question.

"And Mr. Wendon was in his car?"

"No he wasn't." The answer was faint but quite decided.

"How do you know?"

"I know because I looked," said Todman with a renewed spasm of petulant energy. "Wanted to ask him about that account of his—been waiting long enough for it. Car in the park, under the trees. Wasn't no sign o' Wendon. No sign. No signal. Like that bloody cyclist. He never gave no signal. They're all the same—push-bikes and motor-bikes. No signals. You ask Mrs. Pink what I did to her bike. She…"

"That will do," said the sister firmly.

"Where are we going to now?" said Sergeant Broome, as the Superintendent's car turned on to the by-pass road that, avoiding the narrow streets of Markhampton, led northwards up the vale of the Didder.

"Druids Hotel," Trimble answered briefly. They were the first words he had uttered since leaving the hospital.

Broome shrugged his shoulders philosophically and turned once more to the difficult task of writing up his notebook in a car that was being driven at speed.

They found Humphrey Rose sitting in a deck-chair on the lawn behind the hotel under a copper-beech tree. The customary cigar was in his mouth and he was reading *The Financial Times*. He did not get up when the detectives approached but nodded to them in a friendly and slightly patronizing fashion over the top of his newspaper, which he did not bother to put down.

"Mr. Rose," said Trimble, "have you any objection to answering a few more questions on what you said to me yesterday?"

"Not the slightest," said Rose genially.

"Then perhaps you would come into the hotel with us for a few moments."

Rose looked meditatively round the garden. The only other occupants were an elderly couple sitting together on a rustic seat well out of earshot. He looked up to the sky, which was a pure unclouded blue.

"Thank you very much," he said, flicking the ash off his cigar, "but I am quite comfortable where I am."

There being no other seat within sight, the officers were left with the choice of sitting on the ground or remaining standing—the choice, in other words, between crouching at the feet of their suspect like disciples before their teacher, or standing in front of his chair, like servants receiving orders. It was the kind of calculated rudeness at which Rose was particularly adept. Trimble recognized it for what it was and mastered his temper only with difficulty.

"Very well," he said. He looked at the grass, realized that it was slightly damp, and decided on the more tiring though less undignified alternative. "I have just come from interviewing Mr. Todman," he went on, staring down into Rose's untroubled face.

"Todman? Ah, yes, the garage proprietor. A very temperamental driver. Did I tell you, by the way, that he tried to run my poor wife down with his car the other day? The Ransome boy will tell you about it if you are interested."

"Todman," Trimble continued doggedly, refusing to be sidetracked, "Todman took your luggage up to The Alps on Thursday, leaving you to walk up the hill."

"So he did. But we've been into this before, surely?"

"What we have not been into before, Mr. Rose, is this—if you were walking up the hill as you say, why did not you and he see each other when he was driving back down the hill?"

Rose shook his head gravely.

"Certainly you ought to have thought of that yesterday, Superintendent," he said in a reproving tone.

"I am asking you now, did you see Todman's car coming down the hill?"

"If Todman came down direct from The Alps, and if I happened to be looking in his direction at the moment, no doubt I did."

"Then it was his car you saw and not Wendon's?"

"You seem to jump to conclusions in a most irresponsible fashion. I haven't said that I didn't see Wendon's car." Rose yawned slightly and glanced down at the newspaper in his hands.

"Listen, Mr. Rose. I don't think you are attending properly to what I am saying. Todman tells me that he saw you on the brow of the hill. He tells me further that Wendon's car was not on the road at that moment at all, but standing in the car-park at the top, unoccupied. If that is correct, it follows that you could not have seen it on the road, because once over the brow you are out of view of the road. Do you follow me?"

"Perfectly. What I understand you are trying to convey, in a rather muddled fashion, is that Todman tells one story and Wendon another."

"I have not said anything about Wendon's story," said Trimble, by now thoroughly nettled. "I am concerned with yours."

"My story, if I am to call it that, did not mention Wendon, if my recollection is correct."

"It mentioned a car which was readily identifiable with his."

"Quite right."

"And that was in answer to a question of mine after you knew I had seen Wendon at the police-station."

"Quite right," repeated Rose amiably.

"I suggest that you invented that answer so as to agree with Wendon's statement."

Rose raised his eyebrows.

"It would have been very clever of me to have guessed what

it was that brought Wendon to see you yesterday," he observed.

"I think you are a very clever man, Mr. Rose."

Rose nodded his head. "Yes, I am," he acknowledged.

"If Todman is telling the truth your answer was a complete fabrication."

"So it would appear."

"For the last time, Mr. Rose, are you prepared to tell me whose car it was you saw on the hill?"

Rose blew a fragrant cloud of smoke through his nostrils and very deliberately ground the butt of his cigar into the grass beside his chair.

"No," he said, "I am not. On reflection, I am not prepared to say whether I saw any car at all. As I suggested just now," he went on before the disgusted Superintendent could interrupt, "you are really asking me to determine between the truth of what you tell me Todman says and what, as you suggest, I am clever enough to guess that Wendon says. Now, I am not a policeman, and it is a matter of complete indifference to me which of these two unimportant individuals is telling the truth— if either of them are. As you will already have observed, I am not particularly interested in truth as an abstract principle. I am interested in one thing, and one thing only, and that is"—he spoke deliberately and with long pauses between the words— "saving—my—own—neck." He let the crude phrase sink in before he went on in his usual measured tones, "You told me yesterday that there was only my word to vouch for the fact that I was in a particular place at a particular point of time. It now appears that I have the word not of one but of two independent witnesses to support my story. That is quite good enough for me. The fact that they are so independent that their accounts are mutually inconsistent does not worry me in the least. It is sufficient for me that between them they make it completely impossible for anybody outside Bedlam to think of prosecuting me. Have I made myself clear?"

Rose extracted another cigar from his case, cut it with a gold cigar-cutter and lighted it. He then looked up at the detective still glowering speechless before him, gave what could only be interpreted as a nod of dismissal, and opened his newspaper with a flourish. When Trimble looked back across the lawn he could see only the white sheets of paper extended wide, a thin column of blue smoke rising above them, and, beneath, the beautifully trousered legs of Humphrey Rose, stretched out in comfortable relaxation.

20

Two Shocks for Pettigrew

"You ought to have told me about this before," said Pettigrew reproachfully.

"Well, sir," Godfrey told him, a touch of defiance showing through his evident distress, "you didn't exactly encourage me to go into details when I spoke to you the first time, did you? You seemed so positive that I had nothing to worry about, and——"

"I know. I know," Pettigrew groaned. "I was too cocksure altogether. I took things for granted on incomplete data. It's so easy to do that with other people's affairs. As What's-his-name says: 'Courage in another's trouble, kindness in one's own.'"

"I don't think," said Godfrey seriously, "that you've got that quotation quite right."

"Of course I haven't; but I've got it much nearer the facts of human nature than What's-his-name ever did. But this isn't a joking matter. If I'd known about your mother's ear-ring at the time you spoke to me I should never have been so airy-fairy about the whole business. When did the police come to your house this morning?"

"Quite early. We hadn't even finished breakfast."

"Sound psychology on their part. Nobody's at their best at that hour in the morning. I suppose one should be thankful they don't turn up in the small hours, as they do in some countries. You say they were positive your mother lost the thing on Thursday evening?"

"Yes. They'd got that out of Grethe before they started on mother and me. Grethe had noticed one ear-ring was gone when she came in."

"And she came in after Rose turned up at the house?"

"So Grethe said, I gather. I was upstairs in my room, so I couldn't help them about that."

"But you did help them to this extent—that your mother had said she was going out just after Mrs. Pink had left, nominally to meet Rose?"

"Yes...I didn't mean to tell them anything, actually, but it slipped out somehow."

Pettigrew nodded sympathetically. "You needn't excuse yourself," he said. "That was natural enough. Making people slip things out is the business of the police. They are very good at it. Anyhow, your evidence is a minor factor. It's Todman's story that matters. You can be quite sure it was that that brought them back to The Alps."

Godfrey nodded gloomily. "Todman was there all right," he said. "After I'd gone upstairs I saw him out of my bedroom window in his car just outside the front gate."

"Todman is a nasty customer," mused Pettigrew. "Of course he may be lying to save his own skin, but if he is it's a damned inconvenient lie. It fits in too well with the known facts. What had your mother to say to all this?"

"She told the police to go to hell and said she would consult her solicitor."

"I see."

"That was roughly what she said the first time they came, of course. Only—only this time it didn't seem to work so well."

"I think I understand. They assured her that she was quite entitled to take up that attitude if she wished, and of course she

180

need not help the police if she would prefer not to and they wouldn't question her any further. And all the time they went on asking questions that simply had to be answered. Was that it?"

"More or less."

"I think I know the technique. What was the effect of it?"

"It was rather a bad show altogether," said Godfrey reluctantly. "I've never seen Mother really rattled before, and I didn't like it. She's such a calm sort of person as a rule. She told them about half a dozen different stories one on the top of another and couldn't stick to any of them. Whenever she said one thing they just chivvied her out of it into another, like dogs after a rat. It was horrible. First she said she hadn't been out at all. That was no good, of course. Then she said she had been out to meet Mr. Rose. The Superintendent creature pounced on that. He got her to say that she had met him and then that she hadn't, and in the end that she couldn't remember whether she had or hadn't. They got her all muddled up about the different paths on the hill, and all the time they kept coming back to that blasted earring. I thought they were never going to stop. But they did in the end, quite suddenly, and went off looking disgustingly pleased with themselves. I don't think they'd have been so bad if Mother hadn't made them look such fools the first time they came."

"Very likely. And where is your mother now?"

"In bed. At least, that was where she said she was going. She'd hardly let me speak to her after they had gone. She practically turned me out of the house."

"So you came down here. Very wise of you. You'll stay to lunch, won't you?"

"Thanks awfully. Mrs. Pettigrew's asked me to already, as a matter of fact."

"Good! And stay as long as you like afterwards. My wife and I have to go into Markhampton this afternoon, but you can have the run of the garden if you wish, and you can get yourself some tea."

"Thank you, sir. I was wondering, if it isn't awful cheek, do you think I could stay on to supper as well?"

"I dare say that could be managed, but you are sure you oughtn't to be at home by then? After all, your mother has had a pretty nasty experience. She'll be all alone, and——"

"That's just the point, sir. She won't be alone and she won't be at home either. Just before I left I heard her telephoning to arrange to meet Mr. Rose for dinner at the Druids Hotel this evening."

"Oh!" said Pettigrew shortly. He said nothing further for a moment, and then added, "It can't make much difference at this stage of affairs, but it's unpleasant all the same. By that, I am not referring to your dining with us, I may say. Whether the larder will stand it or not remains to be seen. We might perhaps go out for a bite somewhere. But it's a mistake to look more than one meal ahead. I think that lunch is nearly ready. What do you say to a glass of sherry?"

If lunch proved to be not too dismal a meal, the credit was due entirely to Eleanor Pettigrew. Her husband was for the most part silent, preoccupied in his own thoughts, which he was unable or unwilling to share. Fortunately Eleanor, after casting about in several directions, happened to mention that she was going that afternoon to a rehearsal of the Markhampton Orchestral Society, and found that Godfrey was sufficiently interested in music to be able to keep his end up in conversation. A lively if not very profound argument on the merits of Benjamin Britten sufficed to last out the time until the hosts had to take their departure to Markhampton.

Just before they left, Pettigrew, coming suddenly out of his abstraction, took Godfrey into his study.

"I don't know how you intend to spend the afternoon," he said, "but I have a suggestion to make. The fact that it is the precise opposite of what I suggested to you before won't, I hope, deter you from acting on it. Here is a desk, pens, ink and paper. Here is also a magnificent view of Yew Hill. My proposal is that you sit down and, firmly averting your eyes from the view, write down exactly and in detail every single thing you can recollect of what happened from the time that Mrs. Pink arrived at The Alps until you went up to your room. Everything, mind, however trivial. You will find it a quite sickening task, and I can't promise that it will prove to be of the smallest value. But I shall read what you have written when I come back, and it may be that I shall find there——" He paused.

"Find what?" said Godfrey.

"I can't tell you. If I did I should merely be putting ideas into your head, and my whole plan is to get your unaided recollection. But, unless I am really the silly old man you probably think me to be, I know the truth about this case, and it's just possible that without knowing it you can supply the means to prove it. Anyhow, are you ready to try?"

Godfrey said nothing. But he sat down at the desk and before Pettigrew had left the room his shoulders were squared to write.

If Superintendent Trimble was, as Godfrey put it, "disgustingly pleased with himself" when he left The Alps, his pleasure was somewhat diminished by the time that he had finished the conference which the Chief Constable had unexpectedly called later that morning. Mr. MacWilliam was, as always, politely appreciative of the work that had been done, but he was decidedly lacking in enthusiasm.

"What it all boils down to is this, is it not?" he said. "The evidence of the ear-ring, which we have had since the very beginning of the enquiry, suggested that Mrs. Ransome was in the neighbourhood of the crime at about the time it took place. The fresh evidence which you have procured (and on which I should like to congratulate you highly, most highly indeed) does not do more than turn that suggestion into a virtual certainty. The question still remains—is that enough to put Mrs. Ransome on her trial?"

"I—well, I should have thought so, sir."

"Is it? With at least three other suspects hanging about in the neighbourhood? There was time enough for one of them to slip down the hill and dispose of Mrs. Pink before Mrs. Ransome ever came on the scene. Suppose she were simply to say, 'I was there, but didn't see Mrs. Pink or anybody else, so I came straight home again', how is the prosecution, without more, to prove its case? Did she say that when you questioned her, by the way?"

Trimble looked at Broome.

"She said that," the Sergeant put in. "Along with a lot of other things. She told every sort of story she could lay her tongue to, and all of them obvious lies, in my opinion."

"That's just it, sir," Trimble persisted. "You're forgetting, if I may say so, that when she was questioned she told a pack of untruths. About taking the upper path and not the lower, about meeting Rose, when in fact they came in at different times, and so on. That's quite enough to prove her guilty so far as I'm concerned."

The Chief Constable shook his head. "I fear, Mr. Trimble," he said, "that you are in danger of forgetting the great passage in *Taylor On Evidence*."

Trimble, as MacWilliam well knew, was not in the smallest danger of forgetting something of which he had never heard, but in the presence of Sergeant Broome he had to do his best to disguise the fact as his superior reached for a battered volume on the shelf behind him, found the passage he wanted and read aloud:

"*Innocent persons, under the influence of terror from the danger of their situation, have been sometimes led to the simulation of exculpatory facts; of which several instances are stated in the books.*"

"What books?" the Superintendent made bold to ask.

"I haven't the least idea," MacWilliam replied, shutting the volume and returning it tenderly to its place. "I have often wondered; but, as Taylor has been dead a good many years now, I suppose I shall never know. I'm sure his modern editors do not. But that doesn't alter the fact that that sentence should be engraved on every policeman's heart. A lying witness is not necessarily a guilty one. Which brings me to my next point. Are not all our principal witnesses here lying; and if not all, which of them, and why?"

184

The hapless Trimble squirmed in his chair.

"I'm not sure that I follow you, sir," he said.

"My fault entirely. A portmanteau question of that kind is unanswerable. Let's take it by stages. Your case against Mrs. Ransome depends strongly on Todman, does it not?"

"Yes, sir."

"Very well. If Todman is a witness of truth, it follows that Rose and Wendon are both liars. Leave Rose out of it for the moment, why should Wendon want to lie?"

"To give himself an alibi, I suppose, sir."

"Why should he need to, if Mrs. Ransome is the guilty party?"

"I suppose he can simulate an exculpatory fact as well as the next man, sir, can't he?"

"Very neat, Superintendent. I deserved that one. But is that really the position? Wendon wasn't really concerned to give himself an alibi, but somebody else. He never said that Rose had seen him. It was the other way round. And it was Rose—on the footing that Wendon is a liar—who simulated the exculpatory fact to agree with Wendon. Why should Wendon simulate a fact to exculpate someone he hates like poison? Because, mind you, unless he did, Todman's story is an invention and away goes your case against the lady."

Trimble's head was beginning to whirl, but he stuck doggedly to his point.

"I can't see that Todman has any reason for lying," he said.

"I can see every reason for his lying about Mrs. Ransome. He's a man with the strongest possible motive to kill Mrs. Pink— far stronger than hers, and at least as strong as Rose's. (Has anybody thought of any motive at all for Wendon, by the way? At the moment I can see none.) But I agree that there is no known reason why Todman should go out of his way to give Rose an alibi. Has it occurred to you, by the way, what a very lucky fellow Rose is, to have two witnesses tumbling over each other to clear him? After all, with his record and in his position, he's by far the most likely candidate. I don't mind telling you, I

185

want Rose to be the murderer in this case, with or without Mrs. Ransome."

"Excuse me, sir," said Broome diffidently, "but I have an idea. Suppose we have Wendon and Todman both telling lies. That leaves Rose free to come up the hill the other way and help Mrs. Ransome kill Mrs. Pink."

"A beautiful idea," said the Chief Constable sadly. "But unless you can produce something new and startling in the way of evidence, Sergeant, I fear that it is destined to remain in the realm of ideas for ever."

And on that note the conference adjourned for lunch.

Eleanor's rehearsal was to be held in a gaunt drill hall hidden away in a back street behind the market-place. Pettigrew parted from her there with a sharp pang of envy. For an hour or two she would be in a world apart, a world where the values were purely aesthetic, the problems merely technical, a world to which he had no key. The prospect of an afternoon's leisure, for once, appalled him. At once indolent and inquisitive, he did not normally feel the need of any particular object to occupy his mind on his visits to Markhampton. The town itself, so familiar and so picturesque, so charged with historical associations and with memories personal to himself, was ordinarily a quite sufficient entertainment. But on this occasion he felt the need of something to rid his mind of the ugly thoughts that clouded it, and he could find nothing. He passed by the County Court, where Judge Jefferson, restored to health, was even now, no doubt, grappling with some insoluble problem of greater hardship or alternative accommodation, and found himself uncharitably wishing that his illness could have been prolonged indefinitely. He turned into a hairdresser's shop for a much needed hair-cut, and was quite disgusted to find himself attended to at once and turned out, shaven and shorn, into the street again within a bare twenty minutes. He turned into the cathedral, and found that for once that superb building had nothing to say to him. Finally he sought consolation in the haven of the town's one antiquarian bookseller, and busied himself in the musty recesses of the rambling old shop.

He had been there some time, wandering moodily from one shelf to another, taking down volumes only to replace them after the most cursory inspection, when he bumped into another customer who appeared to be similarly engaged on the opposite side of the narrow book-lined corridor in which he found himself. He apologised automatically and moved on. Then a voice behind him said:

"Found anything to interest you?"

Pettigrew turned round and saw the Chief Constable.

"I'm surprised to see you here," he said. "What are you looking for?"

"Pornography," said MacWilliam cheerfully.

"Really! I shouldn't have expected that here. Have you had any luck?"

"It depends what you mean by having luck. I should have said, Yes. You see, I've had a complaint from a lady that this shop is publicly offering for sale lewd and obscene so-called works of literature calculated to deprave the citizens of this town and excite impure thoughts and emotions in the breasts of the younger generation. I think I have quoted her correctly. She did not sully her pen by naming the filthy volumes to which she referred, but she was good enough to indicate exactly where in the shop they were to be found. She must have spent an enjoyable day tracking them down."

"So you have been following in her footsteps?"

"Precisely. It's not work that I care to leave to any of my officers, you'll understand. They are a very good lot of men, but they have their limitations, and to turn them loose among so-called works of literature with a roving commission to hunt for obscenities would be asking for trouble. The English," said MacWilliam, a trace of Highland accent appearing for once in his speech, "are not by and large an educated people."

"Very true. No more than the Scotch or the Irish or the Welsh, I expect. But putting that aside, what have you found?"

"What I expected. All the old friends of the smut-hound.

Rabelais, *The Decameron*, Restoration dramatists, *Tristram Shandy*, and a rather nice translation of Apuleius, which I intend to buy for myself. That will be one source of depravity removed from the citizens of Markhampton, at any rate. They will have to take their chance with the rest, so far as my force is concerned. And what about you, sir? Have you found anything interesting?" He looked down at the volume in Pettigrew's hands. "You're reading the trial of Adelaide Bartlett, I observe."

"Am I?" said Pettigrew absently, and returned the book to its place.

"They've got a good collection of old trials," MacWilliam remarked, glancing up at the shelf. "They interest you, I expect?"

"Not particularly, if you mean trials for murder. There is more real drama, to my mind, in a really hard-fought action over a disputed will, say, than in half of these sordid affairs. Still, there are exceptions. I may be wrong, but I think that the murders of my youth were more exciting than any we get today. Take Crippen, for instance. What fun that was!"

"Crippen," repeated the Chief Constable absently. "Crippen! Yes—the chase across the Atlantic and all that. Crippen!" he said yet again, and this time there was a gleam of interest in his eyes. "There was an action about *his* will, wasn't there?"

"Yes, there was. Quite an interesting one, in its way, too. But why do you——"

"By God!" said MacWilliam suddenly. "I believe I've got it!"

He seized Pettigrew by the arm in a grip that made him wince.

"We can't talk in here," he said rapidly. "Where shall we go? I know, the County Club opposite—you're still a member, aren't you? It's bound to be empty at this time of day. Slip across there now and I'll follow. I don't want my Superintendent to see us together. As soon as I've paid for my Apuleius I'll join you. Don't argue, man, go! If you don't help me now I'll arrest you for obstructing the police! Crippen! Why on earth didn't I think of him before?"

21

At the Druids Hotel

"An intelligent man, the Chief Constable," Pettigrew remarked to his wife, as they walked together up the lane from the railway station to their home.

"Do you say that because he doesn't think the classics obscene, or because he came to the same conclusion as you did, Frank?"

"Neither, although I should be quite prepared to argue that they are both signs of intelligence. So far as I was concerned, I made a guess, on quite incomplete data. The Chief Constable, with all the facts in front of him, had already toyed with my theory, but saw what seemed to be a fatal objection to it. When, quite unconsciously, I gave him the answer, he tumbled to it at once. From no more than the barest hint, he was able to see that what had looked like an argument against the case was the strongest possible support to it. It was very impressive."

"So everything is all right?"

"I wish I could say that, but it isn't. There's a long step between being morally certain who committed a crime and being able to prove it. At the moment I'm blowed if I can see how that step's going to be taken." Pettigrew opened the front door of the house and looked around. "I wonder where that boy's got to?" he observed.

In the kitchen the tea-things had been neatly washed up and stowed away. On the study desk was a small pile of manuscript. Of Godfrey there was no trace.

"Odd!" said Pettigrew. "He particularly asked to be allowed to stay to supper. He must have changed his mind and gone off somewhere."

He sat down at the table and began to look through what Godfrey had written. He had only read a short way when he exclaimed, "By George! This is really interesting! Listen, Eleanor——"

Turning round, he saw that Eleanor was no longer in the room. He finished reading Godfrey's script, without finding anything else calling for remark, and then returned again to the passage which had attracted his attention. He was still brooding over it when his wife came back. He saw with surprise that she was wearing an overcoat.

"Where are you going?" he asked.

"I am going to the Druids," said Eleanor firmly. "And if you want anything to eat this evening you are coming too. There is nothing in the larder but a disgusting collection of remnants, and after working hard all this afternoon I absolutely refuse to consider trying to turn them into anything worth sitting down to."

"You've certainly earned an evening out," said Pettigrew. "Let it be the Druids, by all means. But what about young Ransome? Should we wait for him, in case he comes back?"

"He is quite old enough to look after himself. In any case, I don't think I should be called upon to make conversation with him at two meals running."

"I'm afraid I wasn't very helpful at lunch. Not nearly so helpful as this boy has been to me. Just listen——"

Eleanor took her husband by the shoulders and shook him vigorously.

"We are going out to dinner," she said. "With dinner I shall expect a bottle of something good. Before dinner we are going to have several expensive drinks in the bar. After dinner we shall have coffee and liqueurs. During the whole of that time we are not going to talk or even think about this disgusting, sordid, atrocious affair that has made my life a misery for the last two weeks. Now put those papers away and go and get your hat and coat."

"Very well, my love," said Pettigrew meekly. He tidied up his desk, noticing as he did so that his field-glasses were not in their usual position. He replaced them, mechanically adjusting the focus to suit his own eyesight. Evidently Godfrey had not been proof against the temptation that they afforded. "I promise not to say a word about the murder this evening, unless——"

"Unless what?"

"Never mind. I was thinking of a very remote contingency. Let's go."

"No," said Humphrey Rose, sipping his cocktail appreciatively. "No, Marian, decidedly not. I shall not say any such thing." He accompanied his refusal with a smile so charming that anyone watching him from a little distance—the barman at the Druids Hotel, in this case—would have thought that he was conferring a favour. "Let me get you another glass of sherry," he added.

"I don't want another glass of sherry," said Mrs. Ransome tersely. "I simply want you to tell anybody who asks you that you met me on the hill that evening and that we came in together."

"You have explained that already. Don't make me have to refuse twice. It is such a waste of effort. You would be much better employed looking at the menu and deciding what we should eat."

"Do you realize that unless I can get some sort of evidence to back me up I may be arrested at any minute?"

"All the more reason to make sure of a good meal while you can. The cooking in prison is, I can assure you, a disgrace."

"What's to prevent my saying that I saw you in the Druids' Glade with your wife that night? I certainly shall if I'm questioned again."

"Nobody will believe you, Marian, that's the beauty of it from my point of view. I have the good fortune to possess two witnesses of unimpeachable character to say that I was nowhere near her. It's a pity that you are not so lucky, but I'm not going to throw away my own security by indulging in any mistaken altruism."

"You know as well as I do that the truth of the whole matter is——"

"I'm not in the least interested in the truth," said Humphrey Rose. He spoke with the simple sincerity of a man avowing a deeply cherished principle of conduct.

"Humphrey," said Mrs. Ransome, her voice hardening and rising a semitone in pitch, "I always knew you were a double-crossing little rat, but——"

"Please don't let us have a brawl in here. I have a certain reputation to sustain here in this place. Besides, there's someone coming in....It's my creditor-witness, your egg-merchant friend. Would you like to go and have a chat with him, Marian?"

"No, thank you."

"Just as you please." They were sitting at a small table, and Horace Wendon, standing at the bar, had his back to them. Rose looked interestedly while Wendon's order was given and consumed. "Two double whiskies in quick time," he observed. "Both paid for in ready money! Our friend is fairly flush for once, I'm glad to see. I owe him a lot."

"How many thousand pounds was it exactly?" asked Mrs. Ransome bitterly.

"Bless me," said Rose with a jovial laugh, "I wasn't thinking of *that!*"

Two more patrons entered the bar at this moment.

"That elderly type looks familiar," Rose observed. "A lawyer, if I'm not mistaken. I suppose the mousey little woman with him is his wife. She must be years younger than he. Well, Marian, if I can't persuade you to have another drink we might as well go into dinner. I thought of ordering——" He broke off abruptly as the sound of a furious altercation made itself heard in the back regions behind the bar. Violent imprecations in French and broken English mingled with quieter but penetrating official tones and the clatter of pots and pans. There was a crash of splintering crockery. "There seems to be some trouble in the kitchen," Rose remarked.

Trouble in the kitchen there undoubtedly was; and trouble, moreover, at the very moment when a kitchen should be at its peak of concentrated efficiency—just before the first service of dinner was due to begin. As might have been expected, a convulsion in the nerve-centre of the hotel was not long in communicating itself to its outlying parts. First the head-waiter, then the manager appeared, flitted hastily across the scene and vanished in the direction of the disturbance. There was a pause, during which the noise died down, only to assert itself once more.

"It seems as though our dinner might be delayed," Pettigrew murmured to Eleanor.

"I expect it is just the chef being a little temperamental," she said hopefully.

"Possibly. But, unless I've forgotten all my French, it sounds rather more serious than that." He cocked an ear towards the hotel entrance. "Excuse me one moment, I just want to see…"

He walked quickly out of the bar and was absent for less than half a minute. When he came back there was a rather grim smile on his face.

"I thought so," he said. "The place is chock-a-block with police."

He spoke sufficiently loudly for everyone in the room to hear. Mrs. Ransome stiffened in her chair, her face a sudden mask of chalky-white. Rose was smiling still, looking down at the empty glass in his hand. But there was something fixed and unnatural in his smile, and his gaze was as vacant as the glass itself.

Wendon did not move from where he stood hunched up over the bar, but he ordered another double from the imperturbable barman and raised it to his lips with a shaking hand.

"I met someone else outside," Pettigrew went on, "and asked him to join us. He was in rather a mess, so I sent him to wash his hands. Here he is."

"Godfrey!" exclaimed Mrs. Ransome in surprise.

Her son took no notice of her, but walked across to where the Pettigrews were standing.

"Good evening," said Eleanor. "We had given up all hope of you."

Godfrey was confused, and for once almost inarticulate.

"I'm awfully sorry," he stammered. "I didn't know you'd be here, of course. I mean—I'm afraid—in a way—all this is really my fault."

"Dinner will be served in a few minutes now, ladies and gentlemen, if you would like to take your places. We apologize for the delay." The head-waiter, flushed but suave, had appeared at the door leading through to the dining-room. Several guests who had drifted in during the last few minutes followed him through with expressions of relief. Mrs. Ransome moved to go, but Rose restrained her.

"Now we are here we might as well see it out," he said. "It all promises to be quite interesting."

"Your fault?" said Pettigrew to Godfrey. "Do I understand that you have set the police on to the unfortunate chef at this place? And if so, why?"

"Well, you see, after I'd finished my writing I thought I'd go for a stroll. I borrowed your field-glasses and——" Looking round, he caught sight of Wendon for the first time. "Oh Lord! This is a bit awkward!" he murmured.

Pettigrew followed his gaze and then gave a sudden shout of laughter.

"Of all the ridiculous anticlimaxes!" he said. "I believe I understand!" He turned to Eleanor. "We might as well go into dinner," he went on. "Godfrey can explain it all while we feed, using the menu as a text."

But before they could move Superintendent Trimble had entered. Sergeant Broome was just behind him. The Chief Constable stood in the doorway leading to the main entrance of the hotel.

"Mr. Wendon," said Trimble, "may I have a word with you?"

Wendon turned round and faced the room for the first time. His weak face was flushed and defiant.

"Yes," he said thickly.

"If you'll just come outside for a moment——"

"I prefer to stay where I am. You can talk to me here."

Trimble's glance travelled past Wendon for an instant, towards the door. There was a barely perceptible nod from the Chief Constable.

"Very well," said the Superintendent, "if you prefer it." He cleared his throat and began to speak as though he was reciting a piece learned by heart. "I have just come from the kitchen premises of this hotel, where I took possession of a portion of freshly killed pork, for which the chef was unable to account. I have reason to believe that you supplied the chef with the pork in question without being in possession of the requisitive licence entitling you to do so. It is my duty to warn you that anything you may say will be taken down in writing and given in evidence."

"Ha! Ha!" said Wendon deliberately.

"What did you say?"

"I said, Ha! Ha! You can take that down in writing and give it in evidence if you like. And you can add this, that if the chef says I gave him the pork he's a bloody liar."

"Then perhaps you would care to tell me what the chef was doing in the vicinity of your farm this afternoon?"

"He wasn't there."

Trimble extended his hand to Sergeant Broome. With the air of a conjurer, the Sergeant produced from somewhere a newspaper, its outer sheets heavily bloodstained.

"The portion of pork in question," Trimble went on, "was wrapped in the newspaper which I now show you. It is a copy of the *Markshire Advertiser* for the week before last and it bears your name in pencil on the outer sheet. That would appear to have been placed on it by the newsagent who delivered it to you. Would you care to explain how this meat came to be wrapped in your newspaper, Mr. Wendon?"

Wendon's defiance evaporated suddenly.

"All right," he said. He looked slowly round the room, taking in all its occupants with a gaze of weary contempt. "I hope you're all enjoying this," he went on, "watching a decent farmer being persecuted by the law. Rose, who's swindled me and others out of thousands of pounds. Mrs. Ransome, who's been only too happy to buy a pound or two of meat on the side. You all look damned virtuous now, don't you? Especially this bloody little prig of a boy—I suppose it was you who were spying on my farm today with field-glasses. I've got you to thank for this, haven't I?"

"Are you prepared to make a statement, Mr. Wendon?"

Sergeant Broome had his notebook at the ready, his pencil poised.

"Yes, I suppose so. Tell me what you want me to say."

Leaning against the bar, Wendon began to dictate to the Sergeant. Then Pettigrew, for the first and last time, took an overt hand in the proceedings. He moved over to the door, taking Godfrey with him, and spoke in an undertone to MacWilliam.

"Thank you, sir," said MacWilliam. "That is just what I wanted. Mr. Trimble, will you oblige me with that newspaper for a moment?" He studied the gory rag for a while and then nodded in satisfaction. He waited until Wendon had finished his statement and Broome had put away his notebook. Then he went up to Wendon and said in a quiet, almost casual manner, "There's another matter I wanted to ask you about, Mr. Wendon. This newspaper was the one you were reading in your car outside

196

The Alps the afternoon you drove Mrs. Pink there—the afternoon that she was murdered, was it not?"

Wendon said nothing. Only a strange, strangled sound seemed to come from the depth of his throat.

"It carries the item about Mr. Rose's presentation of a portrait of Henry Spicer to the local museum. You read that, I think?"

Again there was no reply, but Wendon seemed to be shrinking into himself as though his clothes had suddenly grown much too big for him.

"You knew, of course, that the portrait had been in Mrs. Pink's possession, because you had seen it at her house. She had told you all her furniture was her husband's. It was this paragraph in the paper that told you that Mrs. Pink was Mr. Rose's wife. That was why you decided to kill her."

There was a long and terrible pause, broken only by the sound of Wendon's laboured breathing.

"You killed her, Wendon, all good and innocent as she was, simply because her husband owed you money. Your attempts to recover anything from him had failed because he had transferred all his property to her, and you reckoned that on her death it would revert to him, where you and the other creditors could get at it. You wouldn't have got very much, you know, because you were only one of hundreds with a claim on the estate. Do you know that if she had been allowed to live it was Mrs. Pink's intention to repay you your debt in full because she was sorry for you? Eight thousand pounds you lost, Wendon, just because you were greedy and callous, when it was there for the taking all the time."

And then Horace Wendon spoke.

"It's not true!" he gasped. "Tell me it isn't true! Eight thousand three hundred and fourteen pounds! She was going to give it to me? Oh, my God! What have I done?"

"I haven't quite finished yet," MacWilliam went on remorselessly. "You might have got away with it, you know, if you hadn't chosen to tell a very obvious lie. But it was a lie you thought you

197

had to tell if you were to collect the fruits of your crime. When you thought that Mr. Rose had been arrested you came forward with evidence to clear him—evidence that was quite unnecessary, as it turned out, because there was a truthful witness who said the same thing. Shall I tell you why you did that? It was because you realized that of all people in the world Rose was the only man you couldn't afford to have convicted of his wife's murder. You knew that if he was, neither he nor his estate could inherit anything from her. You would be left where you started, with a penniless debtor. I give you credit for intelligence in realizing that, Wendon, but it was a fatal lie, none the less."

Pettigrew murmured something to himself. Eleanor, standing beside him, was the only person to hear what he said, and what she heard mystified her completely.

But Wendon did not even murmur. With a look of utter despair he tottered slowly forward. Trimble caught him by one arm and Broome by the other, and, dragging his feet as he walked between the two, he allowed himself to be led away, unresisting.

"Frank," said Eleanor, "what did you mean by what you said just now?"

"I wasn't aware that I had said anything."

"Just before the policemen took him away I distinctly heard you say something. It sounded just like—*Crippen*."

"If that was what it sounded like, then that was certainly what it was."

"But what on earth could Crippen have to do with it? I know all about him—everybody does. He poisoned his wife for the love of Miss Le Neve, and dressed her up like a boy—Le Neve, I mean—and took her to America. And then Scotland Yard sent a wireless message to the ship, and——"

"Quite right. As you say, everybody knows about Crippen. But not everybody knows all about Crippen. Unluckily for Wendon, the Chief Constable does."

"Well, I wish you'd tell me what there was about Crippen that made him in the least like Mr. Wendon, because I simply don't see it."

"There is no resemblance whatever between Wendon and Crippen beyond the brute fact that they were both murderers. The point is that Wendon was, or rather might have been, rather like Miss Le Neve."

Eleanor turned helplessly to Godfrey.

"You're much cleverer than I am," she said. "Do you understand what all this is about?"

Godfrey shook his head.

"It's quite simple, really," said Pettigrew. "Crippen was hanged for murder, as everybody knows. But what not quite everybody knows is that he made a posthumous appearance in the Law Courts, when Miss Le Neve, to whom he had left all his money, made a sporting attempt to claim it. She failed, for the sad and simple reason that Crippen's money had been Mrs. Crippen's until he made away with her, and the law doesn't allow a murderer to profit by his crime—nor a murderer's estate—*nor*, consequently, a murderer's creditors. That's why I say that if Rose had been convicted of his wife's murder Wendon would have been like Miss Le Neve. The Chief Constable, like everyone else, had been put off by Wendon's insistence that Rose, whom he hated like poison, couldn't be guilty. I happened to mention Crippen in conjunction with disputed wills and he took the hint. That's all."

"So in spite of all your protestations, Frank, you were responsible for clearing this up. The Superintendent will never forgive you."

"Let's hope he never finds out. Actually, my part was a very small one. If any one person is responsible for the arrest, I'm not sure it isn't Godfrey."

"But that's not true, sir," protested Godfrey. "I spotted the pork racket, but I never had the least idea it would lead to anything else."

"I wasn't thinking of that, although the pork affair came in very handy for the police. It was that little holiday task I set you this afternoon that did the trick. You see, after the Chief Constable and I had thrashed out the Crippen business we thought we could see pretty clearly that Wendon must have killed Mrs. Pink simply because she was Rose's wife. But there was one fatal snag: how could we prove that he knew that she was his wife? Unless she had told him, which seemed very unlikely, it seemed that he had no means of finding out. Further he must have found it out very late in the day, for up to the last moment all the evidence was that he was on the most friendly terms with her. That was where you came in, Godfrey. Right at the beginning of your account you mentioned that when you took Mrs. Pink into The Alps for tea you left Wendon outside, *reading the local paper*. And that paper, I had reason to know, carried the item about Rose's presenting Mrs. Pink's cartoon of Henry Spicer to the museum. It was when he stumbled on that that he suddenly saw the light. Instead of waiting for your mother he left the eggs with the servant and went off in a hurry to waylay poor Mrs. Pink as she walked down the hill. He's the weak type who would always act on the spur of the moment, I fancy. I had my first chance to tell the Chief Constable about it this evening, and——"

Pettigrew stopped abruptly. "This is dry stuff," he observed. "It may sound callous, but I'm very hungry—and thirsty. Before we go into dinner, though, I've a proposition to put to you, Godfrey...."

"Did you know about this?" Mrs. Ransome was asking Rose meanwhile. Rose nodded.

"As a financier, I naturally looked for a financial motive," he said. "It seemed the obvious one."

"And yet you never said a word! Not even when it looked as if they were going to arrest me!"

"My dear Marian, he was my witness. I couldn't afford to let him down."

"Humphrey, if ever there was a cold, self-centred devil it's you!" The words were bitter, but there was a ring of admiration in her voice.

"Yes," said Rose quietly. He looked at her for a moment, and what he saw in her face induced him to go on. "I ought to warn you, Marian, that I shall really have no money at all from now on. My creditors will take everything."

She nodded. "I know," she said. "But if we live quietly at first—I have just enough for two. And you can't help making some more soon."

"Undoubtedly," said Humphrey Rose. "And until I do we could live on your ear-rings for a month or two. They can't have very pleasant associations for you now."

Mrs. Ransome shuddered. "I must have been within a yard or two of her body when I stopped under the yew tree," she said. "A minute earlier and I should have seen her with Wendon. I might have saved her life."

"Or lost your own," said Rose placidly. "It's no use jobbing backwards, in life or markets. Shall we have another drink?"

They were just finishing their drinks when Godfrey came rather stiffly over towards them.

"Mother," he said, "Mr. and Mrs. Pettigrew have asked me to stay with them for the rest of the holidays. There's only a week left, and I thought on the whole it might be a good arrangement."

"Of course, dear," said Mrs. Ransome with a sweet smile. "Thank them for me, will you? I'll have your things sent down tonight."

The two parties followed each other into the dining-room and sat down at tables on opposite sides of the room.

"Pork is off," said the waiter.